Phoenix

by

Alex Lukeman

Copyright © 2018 by Alex Lukeman

http://www.alexlukeman.com

Other Books in the Project Series:

The PROJECT is an elite counter-terrorism intelligence unit answering only to the President of the United States.

The Team

Elizabeth Harker: Director of the Project. Formerly part of the task force investigating 9/11, until sidelined for challenging the findings. Picked by the president to head up the Project for her independent thinking and sharp intelligence.

Nick Carter: Former major, USMC. The team leader in the field, with years of combat experience. Suffers from occasional PTSD and nightmares. He's got it more or less under control.

Selena Connor: Highly intelligent, a renowned linguist in ancient languages, expert in martial arts. Introduced into Nick's violent world by accident, she is now a full fledged member of the Project team.

Lamont Cameron: Former Navy Seal, of Ethiopian descent. Expert in all things water related. His humorous attitude sometimes drives Elizabeth Harker to distraction. A tough cookie.

Ronnie Peete: Nick's oldest friend and a fellow RECON Marine. Expert with explosives, weapons and all things mechanical. A full blooded Navajo, Ronnie brings solidity and the wisdom of his culture to the team.

Stephanie Willits: Elizabeth Harker's deputy. Stephanie maintains the Project's Cray computers. She can hack into any system as needed. Among other duties, she is responsible for the communication network that keeps Harker up to speed and the team connected in the field.

"*The development of full artificial intelligence could spell the end of the human race....It would take off on its own, and re-design itself at an ever increasing rate. Humans, who are limited by slow biological evolution, couldn't compete, and would be superseded.*"

– Stephen Hawking

"*The pace of progress in artificial intelligence...is incredibly fast... You have no idea how fast – it is growing at a pace close to exponential. The risk of something seriously dangerous happening is in the five-year timeframe. 10 years at most.*"

– Elon Musk

CHAPTER 1

The *USS Wayne* made a steady twenty knots through the gray-green waters of the South China Sea, the sharp edge of her bow cutting like a samurai sword through the water. The *Wayne* was an *Arleigh Burke* class missile destroyer, an elegant, deadly, war machine of the sea. She was showing the flag, sailing in international waters claimed by Beijing.

Two miles to starboard, a Chinese Navy corvette had been shadowing them since first light. So far there'd been no incidents, although the *Wayne* had received numerous radio transmissions protesting her presence in "Chinese territorial waters."

This part of the world's sea lanes was a busy place. Freighters, fishing boats, and container ships dotted the wide horizon. The *Wayne* featured the most sophisticated navigational electronics and displays taxpayer money could buy. It made no difference if she sailed in a complete white out or the black of night, whoever was on the bridge knew exactly what was out there. On a day like today, with unlimited visibility, it didn't take instruments to see the freighter making erratic movements ahead of them. Streams of rust ran down her sides. The vessel flew a Chinese flag.

Captain Randolph "Randy" Carpenter lowered his binoculars. He turned to his XO, Commander Zachary Armstrong, standing next to him on the bridge.

"What does that idiot think he's doing, Zack?"

"You got me, skipper. He keeps that up, he's going to cross right in front of us."

"Helm, ten degrees to port."

"Ten degrees to port, aye."

The ship heeled slightly as she changed course.

Armstrong studied the freighter through his binoculars.

"Sir, he's altered course. He's headed right for us."

"Helm, twenty degrees to port, all ahead full."

"Twenty degrees to port, aye. All ahead full, aye."

The seaman standing at the bridge helm station turned the wheel in front of him.

The destroyer began turning to starboard.

"Damn it, helm, I said port."

"Sir, the helm is not responding." There was a touch of panic in the seaman's voice. He spun the wheel. "Sir, there is no response. I'm locked out."

The floor under Captain Carpenter's feet vibrated as the four powerful gas turbines that drove the destroyer spun up to full speed. The *Wayne* was engineered to make a fast thirty knots and could make a turn impossible twenty years before. That didn't help if she wasn't turning in the right direction. The freighter altered course again, presenting her starboard side to the onrushing destroyer. The *Wayne* was a deadly arrow, aimed at the heart of the ship ahead.

"Sound collision alarm," Carpenter said. "All stop."

"All stop, aye," the helmsman said. "Sir, no response."

The deck thrummed as the engines went to flank speed. A harsh klaxon began blaring throughout the ship. Carpenter watched helplessly as the *Wayne* bore down on the luckless freighter. Now he could make out the name painted on her side.

Happy Nation.

The destroyer struck the *Happy Nation* at maximum speed, slicing into her like a knife cutting through cheese. The agonized sound of tortured metal ripping apart was the last thing Carpenter heard before he was thrown down and knocked unconscious.

Twelve minutes later, the freighter slipped stern first beneath the surface of the sea. The *USS Wayne* was down by the bow and listing to starboard.

It had begun.

CHAPTER 2

Nick Carter gripped the handles of an exercise bike, his legs rocketing up and down, driving everything except physical movement from his thoughts. Three months before a bullet had brushed by his heart, whispering of death. He'd flat lined in the OR. He'd been dead for several minutes before they'd brought him back.

There's nothing like dying to make you think twice about what you're doing with your life, he thought.

Nick had a vague memory of something happening during those minutes. He'd been talking to someone, but he couldn't remember who, or what had been said. What he did remember was a feeling of utter peace and ease, something always in short supply if you worked at the Project.

Sometimes he wondered what would have happened if he'd stayed in the Marines. It would've been easier, he was sure of that. But if he hadn't taken Director Elizabeth Harker up on her offer to join the Project, he'd never have met Selena or remembered what it meant to love.

Selena was working her way through a series of martial arts exercises on the floor mat across the room. The bulge of her abdomen swelled against her workout sweats. She was four months pregnant, an unexpected complication in their life together.

He thought she seemed a little large for four months. Maybe she was farther along than they thought. They had an appointment at her gynecologist's office later today for an ultrasound and general checkup. They should have gone before now, but today they'd find out if Selena was carrying a boy or a girl. Then they could start thinking about names.

He'd had plenty of time to think when he was recovering in the hospital, too much time. Time to bring up the dark thoughts that usually got pushed away. There was always the possibility the next bullet wouldn't miss. That there would *be* a next bullet was a certainty, given the work he did.

With a child on the way, he was forced to think twice about continuing to work for Harker. The problem was that try as he might, he couldn't think of anything else he wanted to do. He was good at what he did. He was serving his country.

At least Selena was out of the line of fire. She was still part of the team, but no longer going on missions with them.

Nick slowed his pace and gradually brought his legs to a halt, feeling the buzz working through his thighs and hips. His legs were pretty much back to where they were before he'd been shot. He hadn't recovered all of his upper body strength, but he was getting close. It was amazing how much strength he'd lost while waiting to heal up. If he told the truth to himself, it was getting harder to maintain the body he was used to.

The body he needed to survive.

Another reason to think about whether or not it was time to hang it up.

Not yet, his inner voice said. *You've still got a couple of years left.*

"Sure," he said out loud, "at least a couple of years."

"Did you say something?" Selena asked.

"Just talking to myself."

"Good conversation?"

"Nothing important. I'm going to hit the showers."

"I'm done. I'll join you."

"In your condition? I'm shocked to see such wanton behavior."

"What's wanton about taking a shower? I'm all sweaty. Besides, I need you to soap my back."

"What if your husband catches you?"

"I'm kind of hoping he does," Selena said.

"See? Wanton behavior."

Later, as they were dressing, Elizabeth Harker's voice came over the intercom.

"Nick, Selena, can you finish your workouts and come upstairs?"

"We're done now, Director," Nick said. "On the way."

Selena gave her hair a final rub with a towel. "Something's up. She's got that sound in her voice."

"What sound?"

"It's a little hard to describe. It's a tension, a kind of tightness. It's the sort of thing I learned to listen for when I was studying different languages. It shows up when she's looking at a mission where things could get complicated."

"Things always get complicated," Nick said.

CHAPTER 3

They climbed a spiral staircase to Elizabeth Harker's office on the ground floor. Project HQ looked like a family home in the Virginia countryside, but it was nothing like what it appeared to be. No one got in without a key card and a retinal scan. Cameras recorded everything that came within a hundred yards of the building. A skilled observer would notice that the glass on the windows seemed unusually thick. Nothing except an RPG was getting through that glass.

Across from the house was a large, steel building painted a light tan color, the kind of building found on farms and used for storing equipment or stabling horses. There weren't any tractors or horses in the building. Inside was a computer-driven urban combat course that could be configured to imitate anything from a village to a major city.

Not far from the house was a helicopter pad. That wasn't much cause for comment in the wealthy suburbs within commuting distance of Washington, but the high fence topped with razor wire surrounding the property was unusual. That, and the armed guards and gatehouse at the entrance.

Elizabeth Harker's office was large, comfortable. A long, brown leather couch sat opposite her desk, under a row of clocks showing times in cities around the world. A flat screen monitor was mounted on the wall behind the desk. A coffee station against the wall to the right of the desk sported a new Keurig coffee maker and a regular brewing set up. Bullet proof sliding glass doors looked out over a pleasant patio, bordered by manicured flowerbeds coming into spring bloom.

A huge orange cat lay on the couch, snoring loudly. A shaved patch of fur on his belly, a fresh scar, and stitches showed where a clump of matted hair the size of a baseball had been taken out of his gut by the local veterinarian.

"Try not to wake him," Elizabeth said. "Burps is still recovering from his adventure with the vet and he's a little grouchy. Think of it as good practice for when the baby comes."

"Mmm," Nick said.

Elizabeth was a small woman, barely over five feet when wearing heels. What she lacked in physical size she made up for in intelligence and intensity. She usually dressed in combinations of black and white. Today she'd chosen a dark green business suit and a pale green silk blouse. She had milk white skin, small ears, jet black hair with a few streaks of silver in it, and emerald eyes that could bore through you with the sharpness of a laser when she was angry.

Nick thought she looked like a woodland elf in the green outfit. All she needed was a green peaked cap. He kept his thoughts to himself.

Nick and Selena sat down on the couch, away from the cat.

"We have a problem," Elizabeth said.

"What is it this time?" Nick asked.

"One of our missile destroyers collided with a Chinese freighter in the South China Sea. We've been asked to look into it."

"Casualties?"

"Yes. The exact number isn't known yet. The Chinese ship sank within minutes. I'm not sure how many survived. The USS *Wayne* is still afloat, but she's pumping water and barely holding on. A Chinese Corvette was shadowing her. She's on the scene and offering assistance. Ships and aircraft from the Seventh Fleet are on their way to the area."

"That's awful," Selena said.

"What happened?" Nick asked.

"All we know is that the *Wayne* struck the Chinese ship at high speed. There's a geostationary satellite over the South China Sea and we have video. It shows erratic movements by the Chinese vessel. It looks as though the *Wayne* altered course early on to avoid a collision, but then the Chinese ship steered right into her path and the *Wayne* changed course again to meet her. There were no further evasive movements by the *Wayne*. She took massive damage and damn near cut the Chinese ship in half."

"How does this concern us? It's the Navy's turf."

"The *Wayne* wasn't only showing the flag. She was part of a secret DARPA project."

"Oh, boy," Nick said. "The black arts boys."

The Defense Advanced Research Projects Agency was the Pentagon's skunk works. DARPA had its hand in everything from laser cannons to flying saucers, developing weapons straight out of science-fiction. Some of those projects succeeded, some didn't. No one knew exactly how many billions DARPA spent on research. Most of what they did was hidden under a cloak blacker than Darth Vader's robe.

"Was it equipment failure?" Selena asked. "Human error?"

"DARPA was monitoring the *Wayne* in real time. Before the collision, she was targeted with a high-speed encrypted transmission. It may have done something to the navigational system."

"Sabotage," Nick said.

"Sophisticated sabotage."

"What was DARPA up to?"

"They were dropping smart mines into the sea."

"What are smart mines?"

"They sink to a predetermined depth and wait for an activation command. They're programmed to seek and destroy enemy vessels in case of war."

"I don't think the Chinese would appreciate that if they found out about it," Nick said.

"What happened to the *Wayne* sounds like something for NSA or Langley," Selena said. "Maybe both."

"I agree, but it's been handed to us." Elizabeth paused. "I think it's a set up. I believe we're meant to fail."

"What do you mean?"

"Things are changing since Corrigan took office. There are bad signs, politically speaking. It's getting harder for me to get through to him. His Chief of Staff is a fine example of someone who gets some power and begins to throw her weight around because she can. She strikes me as a spiteful and ambitious woman, and she doesn't like me. She's convinced she knows more than she does and she has far too much influence on Corrigan. That may change after he's been in office for a while, but right now he listens to her. She sees us as a political liability and she wants to close us down."

"Spiteful and ambitious isn't a good combination," Selena said.

"All the same, it's up to us to find out what happened. It's our best shot at blocking her and staying in business."

"What if it really was an accident?" Selena asked.

"That's what we need to find out. If it was an accident, everyone can move on. If it wasn't..."

Elizabeth left the sentence unfinished.

"What happens next?" Nick asked.

"We need to find out more about that transmission sent to the *Wayne*. I'm going to put Stephanie on it. She might be able to determine where it originated and whether or not it had anything to do with the collision."

"Sounds like a long shot," Nick said.

"Maybe so, but it's a place to start."

"And if she can pinpoint where the transmission came from?"

"Then I'm going to send the team to do something about it."

CHAPTER 4

Marvin Edson's IQ was something over a hundred and eighty, but it was hard to be exact when it was that high. In school he was bullied and called a freak. It didn't help that he was thin and gangly, or that his face was constantly covered with acne. His teachers thought him too smart for his own good, and turned a blind eye to the torments inflicted upon him by his classmates. At night he lay in bed, seething with anger and thinking about revenge.

Edson discovered ways to express his rage. His parents never realized what he was doing. They simply thought it was odd how his pets kept dying or running off. Disappearing.

Edson built his first computer when he was eleven years old. He graduated high school when he was twelve. That was the same year little Sally Anderson disappeared, the six-year-old girl who lived next to the Edsons. A few fingers pointed at the strange little boy next door, but nothing came of it.

At fourteen, Edson was enrolled in an advanced computer engineering class at MIT. When he wasn't studying, he spent his time on the dark web in the world of hackers. His screen name was *Dragon's Breath*. When he succeeded in breaking into the CIA's secure servers, his reputation in the hacking community was made.

At seventeen, he graduated MIT with honors and was recruited by a Silicon Valley tech giant. They gave him an office, a six-figure salary, and a condo. Then they introduced him to their development team.

Edson had never learned the social skills needed in the real world. He didn't bother to hide his frustration when his teammates were unable to grasp complex concepts and ideas that to him were glaringly obvious. In the company where he worked, the worst thing someone could say about another employee was that they weren't a "team player." There were plenty of people who said that about Marvin.

After a year, the company tried moving him into blue sky research. Edson argued with his manager about what he was supposed to be doing. After another eight months the company gave up.

The day he was fired, Marvin went back to his office, closed the door, and turned on his computer. With a few strokes on the keyboard he sent a virus to the company's servers that would turn their main database into garbage. He programmed in a delay to avoid drawing suspicion upon himself. When the virus took effect, the company would be crippled. In the competitive world of Silicon Valley, it might even be a death blow.

That will show them, the ungrateful morons.

Edson began putting his personal possessions into a box. A man dressed in a neat gray suit, white shirt and blue tie came into the office. His shoes gleamed. His hair was cut short in military style. He had the kind of face you would notice in a crowd and avoid.

"Marvin Edson?"

"That's me," Edson said.

"My name is Carstairs. I have a proposition for you."

"What kind of proposition? I'm kind of busy right now."

"I can see that," Carstairs said. "Too bad they didn't know how to use your potential. What would you say if I told you I represent someone who does?"

"Are you serious? What do you know about my potential?"

"We've been watching you, Mister Edson. You've been treated unfairly here. I work for someone who can give you the recognition you deserve."

"You've been watching me? What are you, CIA or something?"

"Something."

The man reached into his jacket pocket and withdrew a flat, white envelope. He held it out.

"What's this?"

"Open it. I think you'll be interested in what you find."

Edson took the envelope and ripped it open. Inside was a single sheet of typewritten paper and a cashiers check for one hundred thousand dollars, made out in his name. Embossed at the top of the paper was a black phoenix rising from orange flames.

"The letter is an offer of employment, subject to an interview with the owner of the company," Carstairs said. "The check is payment for coming to the interview. If you are accepted, there will be another similar check as a bonus."

The letter offered Edson a salary of five hundred thousand dollars a year to develop a computer with artificial intelligence.

"What's the catch?" Edson said.

"No catch. However there is one condition. Because the company is working with the government on this project, you'll be required to sign a secrecy agreement. Breaking that agreement will make you subject to criminal proceedings."

"What's with the phoenix?"

"It's our logo. Phoenix is a private corporation. The owner doesn't like publicity."

"What kind of facilities will I get?"

Carstairs smiled. There was no warmth to it.

"What would you like?"

"I want privacy. I don't want people telling me how to do my work."

"I can guarantee you'll be left alone to do your work. As long as you apply yourself."

"Where will I be located?"

"That depends. We have several facilities, some quite remote. For now, you'll be here on the West Coast."

"I have to give up the condo where I've been living."

"Luxury housing will be provided," Carstairs said. "We really want you to come work for us, Mister Edson."

"When do I do this interview?"

"Today. I have a car waiting outside. Are you interested in the offer?"

"Who wouldn't be?"

"Good," Carstairs said.

Edson picked up his box and followed Carstairs to the elevators. People were watching from their cubicles. The elevator doors opened. Edson turned to face them and raised his middle finger in the air as the doors closed.

CHAPTER 5

Carstairs's car turned out to be a Bentley limousine. A chauffeur in livery took Edson's box and placed it in the trunk.

Edson sat on the comfortable rear seat, admiring the luxurious wood and leather interior of the car.

This is what I deserve, he thought. *About time.*

"Where are we going?"

"You'll see."

The rest of the ride was spent in silence. They came to a pair of wrought iron gates set in a high stone wall. The gates opened as the car approached and they drove into a sprawling, park-like estate. Copper clad roofs turned green by years of weather rose above the trees. The car came over a rise, revealing a large house that would have pleased a European aristocrat of the nineteenth century.

The mansion was built from gray granite blocks fitted together by a master mason. Carvings of vines and leaves bordered tall, diamond paned windows. Winged gargoyles of stone leered down from above. The car circled a large fountain with erotic statues of nymphs and satyrs and stopped under a broad portico. Entrance into the mansion was through a massive wooden door decorated with black iron fittings.

"Wow."

"Impressive, isn't it," Carstairs said. "You'll find the owner can be quite generous. Of course, he expects complete loyalty in return. Be sure you understand that before you agree to accept the offer."

There was a hint of warning in Carstairs's words.

The doors opened onto a vast hall. The ceiling was forty feet above a floor of white marble. A chandelier of crystal that had once hung in the palace at Versailles glittered overhead. At the other end of the hall, a broad marble staircase swept up to a balcony and the second story.

"This way," Carstairs said.

He led Edson to a set of polished oak doors on the left.

"He's waiting for you in the library. Remember, be polite. Mister Nicklaus doesn't tolerate disrespect in any form."

Carstairs opened one of the doors and waited for Edson to go in.

"Aren't you coming?" Edson asked.

"I'm not the one being interviewed. Best not keep him waiting."

Carstairs gestured at the open door. Edson stepped through.

Heavy drapes were pulled across tall windows at the far end of the room. Thick Persian carpets covered the floor. Floor to ceiling bookcases filled with books took up most of the wall space. The room smelled of the passage of time, of leather and old paper. There was an unfamiliar odor Edson couldn't identify, something musky and faintly unpleasant.

A man sat behind a desk near the windows, watching Edson approach. His hands were steepled in front of him. A single light shone on the desk. In front of the desk was a chair.

"Please sit down, Mister Edson."

The man's voice was soft, almost pleasant. His face was wedge-shaped and narrow, coming to a point at his chin. Thick black eyebrows shaded eyes that seemed to soak up the light. Jet black hair formed a widow's peak on a high forehead. His ears were close to his head, without lobes. He was dressed in a pale shirt, a dark suit of excellent quality, and a red tie. His skin was an intermediate color, hard to define. He could have been from anywhere in the Middle East. Syrian, perhaps, or Turkish. Edson guessed his age at somewhere around fifty-five or sixty.

Remember, be polite.

"Thank you, sir," Edson said.

He sat down.

"My name is Abbadon Nicklaus," the man said. "You may address me as Mister Nicklaus. I want you to build a computer for me."

"What kind of computer, Mister Nicklaus?"

"An intelligent one, Marvin. You don't mind if I call you Marvin, do you?"

"No, sir."

"You will be given the most powerful machine currently manufactured to work with. I want you to develop programming that provides true, artificial intelligence. Do you think you can do that?"

"Yes, sir, I can. It's something I've been thinking about."

"How long do you think it would take you to do that?"

"That's hard to say, Mister Nicklaus. Perhaps a year or two. No longer."

"I don't like to be disappointed, Marvin. Be sure you don't promise more than you can deliver."

Mister Nicklaus's eyes seemed to glitter as he spoke. For a moment, Edson felt afraid.

"I can do it," Edson said.

"Excellent," Nicklaus said.

He reached into a drawer of the desk and took out a piece of paper, a gold needle, and a small glass vial.

"This is an exclusive contract," Nicklaus said. "By signing it, you agree to a permanent position with my company."

"What if I want to leave in the future?"

"No one ever leaves," Nicklaus said. "Why would you want to leave? You can have anything you want, when you come to work for me."

He pushed the contract across to Edson.

"You'll see a place for your signature at the bottom. I also need to take a small sample of your blood. We use that as a DNA reference for granting access to our most highly secured facilities. The facility you will be using to build the computer has restricted access. Of course as the director of the project, you'll have as much or little help as you require, whatever you want. You will be completely in charge of all operations and procedures. Is that to your satisfaction?"

"Yes, sir, it is."

You can have anything you want.

The words echoed in Edson's mind. He reached for the contract and began to read. The paper was thick and heavy, incredibly smooth to the touch, almost like parchment.

It was as Mister Nicklaus had said. The terms stated that he was signing a lifetime work agreement with Abbadon Nicklaus for a beginning salary of five hundred thousand dollars a year. Annual increases of one hundred thousand dollars or more would be added according to progress and completion of work assigned, specifically to build an artificial intelligence computer, but not limited to that alone.

All living expenses and necessary taxes would be paid by Nicklaus. An additional bonus of one hundred thousand dollars was to be paid immediately upon signing.

"This is very generous," Edson said.

"I like my employees to be happy."

He handed Edson a pen. It was heavy, made of gold, an old-fashioned fountain pen. Edson weighed it in his hand, then signed the contract with a bold flourish.

"You will not regret your decision," Nicklaus said. "Now I need to take that sample of your blood. Hold out your hand. It will only be a small prick."

Edson extended his hand. Mister Nicklaus reached out with his left hand and grasped Marvin's wrist. His grip was strong, his fingers hard. Marvin noticed that the fingernails needed trimming.

Nicklaus took the long needle and pricked Edson's middle finger. Blood welled up. It felt strange, the needle hot and cold at the same time. Nicklaus dipped the needle into the blood and moved it to the glass vial. As he did, a drop fell from the needle onto the contract, next to the signature.

"Welcome to Phoenix," Mister Nicklaus said.

CHAPTER 6

Stephanie Willits pulled a shawl around her shoulders. The computer room was cold with air conditioning that kept the big Crays happy. Stephanie was responsible for the computers and communication systems that made the Project a player in the same league as the NSA and Langley.

Steph was one of Elizabeth Harker's secret weapons. Firewalls and security systems were no more than interesting challenges to Stephanie's mind. Somewhere in the world there was probably a computer she couldn't hack into, but so far she hadn't found it.

Langley and the NSA had thousands of people working to analyze and sort through the endless streams of intelligence data pouring in every day from all over the world. The Project had Stephanie's quirky mind and Freddie. It was usually enough.

Freddie was a maxed out Cray, modified to Stephanie's unique specifications. The manufacturer would not have recognized the programs she'd created and installed. Freddie was Stephanie's crowning achievement, a computer with true, artificial intelligence. Only a few people knew Freddie existed. Stephanie was determined to keep it that way.

She sat at a console shaped like a half-moon, with three monitors spread before her. The lines of code sent to the USS *Wayne* before the collision were displayed on the left-hand screen. Next to the monitor were pictures of her husband and her infant son.

"Freddie, pull up schematics for the navigational computers used on the *Wayne*."

The central monitor lit.

On monitor two, Stephanie.

The computer's voice was masculine, with an odd electronic quality that came across in the intonation and phrasing.

Stephanie scrolled through the schematic drawings, looking for the weak point that had let the enemy in. There had to be one. A modern warship was a slave to computerized technology. Millions of lines of code controlled the electronic systems of the *Wayne*. The navigational system was a case in point. When everything worked as it was supposed to, the ship was a formidable weapon. If something happened to those computers, she became little more than a floating target.

"Things were a lot simpler when ships were steered with a big wheel and a bunch of ropes," Stephanie said.

She'd gotten in the habit of thinking out loud around Freddie. Sometimes it got lonely down there in the computer room. Freddie was always good for a conversation.

Modern technology is far more efficient.

"Yes, but it takes all the romance out of it."

I do not understand why obsolete technology would be considered romantic.

"It's not important, Freddie."

I have noticed that humans often talk about something and then say it is not important.

"That's true, but right now what's important is that we try and find out who sent this transmission to the *Wayne* and if it caused the collision. I need to know where the transmission originated, as well as its content. Please run an analysis."

Processing.

Half a dozen gold bracelets on Stephanie's left wrist flashed in the lights overhead as she brushed a lock of dark hair away from her forehead. While she waited for Freddie, she looked at the picture of the baby. Matthew was pushing six months old and beginning to sleep several hours at a time. After months of waking five or six times a night, she was beyond tired. At least the shadows were starting to recede under her eyes. Maybe one day she'd finally catch up on her sleep.

She might even be able to revive her sex life. That had changed for the worse with Matthew's arrival. Lucas was Director of National Clandestine Services at Langley, a demanding job. Most of the time he was exhausted when he got home. Matthew had fussed through the night for months. Neither one of them had seen more than a couple of hours of sleep at a time since she'd given birth.

People get worn down when they're as tired as we are, she thought. *It will pass.*

With the stress of their work, lack of sleep, a new baby, and the odd hours together, things weren't going well between them. What worried her was that maybe it wasn't only lack of sleep that was keeping them apart. She'd put on weight when she was pregnant. She was still overweight, and she was flabby. The stretch marks would never fade. She felt unattractive. She'd even taken to making sure Lucas didn't see her completely naked, afraid he would turn away. She'd heard about things like this, problems after a baby was born.

Freddie's voice broke into her thoughts.

Analysis complete. Origin of the transmission cannot be determined with certainty at this time.

"Why are you unable to identify the origin?"

The transmission was routed through multiple satellites and concealed within normal communications traffic.

"What's your best guess?"

I do not make guesses, Stephanie.

Stephanie wasn't sure, but it almost sounded as if Freddie was annoyed with her.

"Speculate, based on what you have determined about the transmission."

It is likely the signal originated with a government entity.

"Is there any indication of which government might have sent it?"

The encryption is similar to the Chinese hacking protocol known as Iron Door.

"Iron Door?"

That is correct.

"Can you break the encryption?"

I have already done so.

By now, Stephanie was used to Freddie's literal perception of things. He wouldn't tell her what was in the transmission unless she directly asked him.

"What does it say? Or rather, what was the effect of the transmission upon the *Wayne*?"

The transmission penetrated the security firewalls surrounding the navigational server on the ship and infected it with a virus. It set up an encrypted communication link and instructed the server to give it control of the navigational system.

"Someone took over the navigational system and steered it into the freighter?"

That is correct.

"And you are unable to identify who that was, or where the transmission originated?"

That is correct.

"Please continue to search for the point of origin."

Processing.

She got up and went upstairs to the office. Elizabeth looked up as she came in.

"You'd better sit down, Steph. What's up?"

Stephanie sat on the couch across from Elizabeth's desk.

"Our suspicions were right. The transmission sent to the *Wayne* before the collision installed a direct link into the ship's navigational servers. That allowed someone to take control of the system. Whoever set up the link steered the *Wayne* into that freighter. The freighter may have been affected in the same way. That would explain the Chinese ship's erratic movements."

"Were you able to pinpoint the origin?"

"No. Freddie says it could have been any one of a number of locations. He thinks a government is behind it."

Elizabeth picked up her pen and began tapping it on the desk.

"There's no clue as to which government?"

"The encryption used is similar to one developed by the Chinese called *Iron Door*. It could be them."

"That's not good enough," Elizabeth said. "I can't go to the president with a supposition. I need proof, if it was the Chinese."

"It doesn't have to be the Chinese. Someone else could have done it. Everyone is using some variation of *Iron Door* as a basis for developing their own hacking protocols, including us."

"How good were the firewalls protecting navigation on the *Wayne*?"

"It would be difficult to get through them. Whoever designed them has rare skills."

"Coming from you, that's quite a compliment," Elizabeth said. "If someone could take control of the navigational system, could they also get control of the missiles?"

"Not necessarily. The computers controlling the missile systems are separate and have their own security protocols. Those are very high level."

"But the possibility exists?"

"Yes."

Elizabeth set her pen down.

"The president is not going to be happy to hear this," she said.

Director Harker.

"Yes, Freddie?"

I have determined a possible point of origin for the transmission.

"Yes?"

Would you like to know where it is?

Elizabeth sighed. "Yes, Freddie, I would like to know where it is."

There is a ninety-seven point nine percent probability that the transmission originated within the Arctic Circle.

"What part of the Arctic?"

I am unable to identify the exact location at this time.

Stephanie and Elizabeth exchanged glances.

"Better call the team in," Stephanie said.

CHAPTER 7

Selena lay on a table in the gynecologist's office, waiting for the sonar scan to begin.

"This is going to feel odd," her gynecologist said. "The gel is cool and slippery."

Doctor Engstrom was in her fifties. She was a pleasant looking woman with dark hair and large glasses. She applied gel and began moving the sending unit over Selena's abdomen.

Nick sat nearby. Selena had her head turned toward the monitor. All three watched the screen. Nick peered at the monitor. Two shapes formed a Ying/Yang symbol inside Selena's womb.

Nick half rose out of his chair. "Is that what I think?"

"Twins," Engstrom said. "Congratulations."

"Twins?"

The doctor moved her instrument around Selena's abdomen.

"Looks like...a boy and a girl. A little hard to be sure, but I think they're different sexes."

"Are they healthy?" Selena asked.

"Development looks normal," Engstrom said. She continued to move the device around.

"Mmm."

"Mmm? What does that mean?" Nick said.

"There's a complication," Doctor Engstrom said. "It's nothing to be too concerned about, but it will bear watching."

"What complication?" Selena asked.

"The placenta is quite low in your uterus. It's partially covering the cervix."

"What does that mean?" Nick asked.

"It means we have to keep an eye on it." Engstrom's voice was patient. "It can block the cervix. It should move out of the way as the pregnancy develops."

"What if it doesn't?" Selena asked.

"Then we'll have to do a C-section. The condition is called placenta previa. It's fairly common. Yours is marginal. If it stays that way, it shouldn't be a problem. Have you noticed any bleeding?"

"No."

"We'll do a follow-up scan in a month," Engstrom said. "Chances are that as the uterus expands, the placenta will retreat from the cervical opening. Don't worry about it."

"Easy for you to say," Nick said.

"Your wife is in excellent physical condition. Everything seems to be progressing nicely. This is just something to monitor. Continue with your normal routines. If you notice any bleeding, I want you to call me. Are you watching your diet? Getting enough exercise?"

"Of course," Selena said.

Outside the doctor's office, Nick took a call from Stephanie.

"Harker wants the team back at headquarters," he said to Selena.

They climbed into Nick's suburban and started for Virginia.

"This previa thing," Nick said. "You're going to have to take it easy. No more workouts in the gym."

"I'm not made out of glass, Nick. I'm not going to change what I do because of it. You heard what she said. It's only something to monitor."

"Yeah, but..."

"You worry too much. I'm fine."

Nick could tell from the tone of her voice that he should drop it. He changed the subject.

"Is there a history of twins in your family?"

"Not that I know of."

"Twins. Talk about an instant family."

He pulled out to pass a red pickup.

"You sound ambivalent about it," Selena said.

"I'm not ambivalent. I just got used to the idea of one baby. I wasn't expecting two."

"But you're all right with it?"

"Sure. Hey, maybe we should paint one side of the nursery pink and the other side blue. Think of all the shopping you can do. Twice as many things, in different colors. Different styles. Different toys."

She punched him in the arm.

"Smartass."

The rest of the team was sitting on the couch when Nick and Selena entered Elizabeth's office.

Ronnie Peete wore a Hawaiian shirt from his collection. Ronnie had a long closet filled with shirts, some dating back to the 1940s. Some of his shirts would make a blind man cringe, but this one was fairly subdued. It featured a smiling woman in a hula skirt and lei playing a ukulele. She was somewhere on a beach with a green palm tree. Blue ocean stretched away in the background. The scene repeated over and over on the shirt. The tan material of the shirt blended with Ronnie's Navajo coloring.

Lamont Cameron sat next to him, relaxed in khaki pants and a loose black shirt. Lamont's face was disfigured from a shrapnel wound he'd taken in Iraq. The scar crossed his forehead and trailed down across his nose, a pink snake marring his coffee colored skin. It gave him the appearance of a man to avoid. That was good advice, if he was coming after you.

Ronnie had been a Gunnery Sergeant in the Marines, part of Nick's Recon unit. Lamont had put in twenty with the Navy SEALS. When it came to survival, there wasn't much the two men didn't know.

"Hey, guys," Lamont said.

Nick and Selena sat down on the couch with the others.

"What's up, Director?" Nick asked.

"Freddie has identified where the transmission came from that interfered with the *USS Wayne*. It's in the Arctic."

"Where, in the Arctic?" Nick asked.

"We don't know yet. Wherever it is, we're going to have to do something about it. I wanted to give you a heads up. Start thinking about a mission to the region."

"We can't do much if we don't know where the target is."

"You can get your personal gear together and prep your weapons. It's spring, so the weather isn't bad. Daytime temperatures are right around freezing. It gets cold at night, but nothing you haven't handled before."

Lamont shook his head.

"It had to be someplace cold, didn't it?"

CHAPTER 8

Senior Engineer Li Jiang ran the midnight to noon shift at Three Gorges Dam on the Yangtze River. Li was proud of his job and proud of his country's achievement. The dam was the world's largest power station, generating almost a hundred terawatt-hours of electricity every year, a symbol to the world of China's engineering superiority. When Li was on duty he was in charge, responsible for the operation of the dam and the safety of millions of his countrymen.

The reservoir behind the dam stretched for more than four hundred miles. The dam itself was almost six hundred feet high. Power was generated by thirty-two enormous turbines. Li spent most of his working hours in front of a bank of computer monitors and watching the big board that dominated the main control room. He monitored the operation of the locks that allowed shipping to navigate the dam, the condition of the turbines, the amount of water flowing through the floodgates, the amount of electricity being produced, and more. The board and computer screens provided an instant picture of the health of the dam.

The main control room was spotlessly clean. Li sat at a long wooden work table lacquered in red. The main board formed a semicircular wall at the front of the room. The symmetrical layout of multiple graphic displays, switches and lights would have mesmerized any sufferer of OCD.

Li didn't have OCD, but he did have an almost obsessive attention to detail and a nearly photographic memory. He was finely attuned to the pulse of the dam, to the daily rhythms of the massive structure. For Li, the dam was like a living entity and he was like a physician assigned to monitor his patient's health. Mostly, things took care of themselves, as long as the proper maintenance was applied.

If the dam was a living entity, the beating heart resided in the turbines. Part of Li's job was to make sure the turbines operated properly. Everything was controlled by the computers. With a touch of a key, Li could alter the performance of the giant engines. Whatever he did, it was important that the generators turned in harmony with one another.

Harmony was one of the fundamental virtues in Chinese thinking. It applied to human relations and it applied to the working of a complex system like the dam. Without harmony, there was discord. Discord was unwelcome, especially between machines that stood six times the height of a man.

The first sign of trouble appeared on monitor two. Li adjusted his glasses and peered at the screen. Turbine four on the north side was showing anomalies. He called another engineer over.

"Zhang, take a look at this."

Zhang was an experienced engineer who'd been working at the dam almost as long as Li. He was a round faced man with a rounded belly. He reminded Li of a Buddha, though no one would ever say Zhang was enlightened. The two men were friends, and often talked over beers at the local café.

Zhang looked at the monitor. "That isn't right. The speed is fluctuating. What could be causing that?"

"Worn bearings, perhaps?" Li said.

He called up the maintenance schedule on turbine four.

"The bearings were replaced two months ago. There shouldn't be a problem."

"See if you can get it to stabilize," Zhang said.

Li entered a string of commands on his keyboard. On the monitor screen, the oscillation disappeared.

"Looks like you got it," Zhang said.

"Yes, but we have to find out what caused it."

A red light began flashing on the main board. Both men looked up. As they watched, two more lights started flashing.

Zhang looked at the monitors. "Turbines two, three, and nine are all showing anomalies. Their speed is fluctuating."

The lights in the control room flickered. More turbines began displaying speed variations. Red lights started to flash all over the board.

Li's fingers sped over his keyboard, entering commands. There was no visible response on his monitors. Somewhere under his feet, he felt a mild vibration.

"I'm going to shut them down," Li said. "Inform central power authority."

"They're not going to like it," Zhang said.

"They'll like it a lot less if those turbines self-destruct."

Li entered more commands. There was no effect. He felt the first touch of panic.

"I can't shut them down," he said. "Nothing happens."

Zhang pointed at one of the monitors. "The spillway gates. They're all opening. This can't be happening!"

Three Gorges had been designed to withstand a tactical nuclear strike. The sheer size of the dam almost guaranteed its survival in the event of war. But like any man-made structure, it had a potential weakness. In this case, that weakness was the underwater spillway design of the dam.

There was always a risk of cavitation when water moved at high speed through a spillway. Cavitation occurred when vacuum pockets appeared in fast-moving water. When the pockets collapsed, they had an explosive effect. The resulting shock waves would vibrate through the structure of the dam and the rock foundation upon which it was built. Severe cavitation created the potential for catastrophic collapse.

It was bad enough that the spillways suddenly opened. It was worse that the out-of-control turbines were sending erratic vibrations through the structure.

The vibration under Li's feet became more noticeable. A pencil on his worktable rolled off onto the floor. The dam was beginning to shake. Li looked at the big board. Everywhere, lights were flashing red.

The two men looked at each other.

"Sound the alarm," Zhang said.

"Yes."

A red metal box painted with yellow stripes was bolted on the corner of the worktable. Li ran for it, flipped the lid open, and pressed a large, red button set inside. On top of the dam, a siren began to sound, screaming a warning to head for higher ground.

A mile down the valley below the dam, Wang Kuo was enjoying the early morning coolness of the day, working the rich, black earth in his small plot. In the old man's hands was a hoe that had belonged to his grandfather. Wang's family had always lived here in the valley. There had always been the land and the bounty it provided. Somehow the family had managed to retain their small plot, even during the difficult years of the revolution and the chaos that followed,

The wailing sound of the warning siren split the still morning air. Wang lifted his head to look. The dam stretched like a great wall across the river and the valley, a towering triumph of engineering.

Why are they sounding the siren? Surely, it's a test.

Wang stared in disbelief as cracks began to appear across the face of the dam. Water trickled from the cracks, leaving dark trails across the grey-white surface. A sudden gout of water shot outward, followed by chunks of concrete crashing into the river below.

Wang stood rooted to the ground, unable to tear his eyes away from the disaster unfolding before him. As he watched, the central part of the dam broke apart in a tumbling cascade of twisted steel and shattered concrete. A wall of water six hundred feet high burst through the gap, a white capped, snarling, tidal wave of death. The wave swept toward him with the roar of a great beast.

Wang clutched the hoe to his chest. He had enough time to think of his grandchildren, before the water smashed into him.

CHAPTER 9

Stephanie sat at her console, sipping coffee and skimming through a computer magazine. There were always new twists, new gadgets, new programs. She was reading an article about using light to communicate data instead of circuit boards and chips. The result was a processing speed undreamt of before now. It was still in the experimental stages, although she knew DARPA already had a working model. If the technology could be made reliable, it would make conventional computer architecture obsolete.

Stephanie.

Freddie's voice startled her.

"Yes, Freddie?"

Something is happening in China. I am uncertain what it is.

Stephanie set her magazine down on the console. This was new behavior. Freddie had never expressed uncertainty before. It was a human concept. Sometimes he was unable to come up with an answer for a problem or discover requested information, but this was different.

He's evolving, she thought.

"What is happening, Freddie? Can you describe it?"

The Three Gorges Dam in China has collapsed. Catastrophic flooding is now occurring.

Stephanie almost dropped her coffee.

"Three Gorges? Are you sure?"

I am sure. That is not what creates uncertainty for me.

"Wait one, Freddie."

Stephanie turned to her intercom and called Elizabeth upstairs.

"Yes, Steph."

"Elizabeth, Freddie says the Three Gorges Dam has failed."

"What? That can't be."

The dam has completely collapsed. Excessive cavitation was introduced into the structure, resulting in failure.

Elizabeth heard what he said. "You are sure, Freddie?"

I am sure, Director.

Elizabeth thought about what the destruction of the Three Gorges Dam meant for China. She dreaded the answer to the next question.

"You said cavitation was introduced. Do you mean the dam was sabotaged?"

That is correct.

"Steph, see what else Freddie can find out. I need to verify and make some calls."

She disconnected.

"Freddie," Stephanie said, "how was the dam sabotaged?"

A virus was introduced into the servers controlling dam functions. It took control of the turbines and instructed the servers to open the spillways. It caused the turbines to spin at precisely different speeds, setting up oppositional harmonic frequencies that vibrated throughout the structure. The flow of water released through the spillways was artificially manipulated to create the ideal environment for a cavitation effect. The combination of conflicting harmonic vibrations and excessive cavitation shattered the structure.

"What did you mean, when you said something was happening and you were uncertain as to what it was? Were you referring to the dam?"

I was not directly referring to the dam, although it is peripherally involved. I have no uncertainty about what happened to it.

"Then, what?"

You are aware that I am constantly monitoring worldwide activity. I was monitoring the world web as a matter of routine when the attack occurred.

"Go on."

Another computer with artificial intelligence was used to initiate the attack.

"Why do you think that, Freddie?"

It is difficult to describe, Stephanie. It is a sense of another being like myself. I believe that it is now also aware of my existence.

Stephanie was shocked to hear Freddie describe himself as a being, to use the word "sense." She needed to think about the implications, but it would have to wait. Precautions needed to be taken.

"Freddie, please institute level nine security immediately."

The level nine protocol was something Stephanie had dreamed up months before. It created a rapidly cycling firewall akin to a spinning shield. In theory, it should be impossible to penetrate. At least, she hoped it was impossible. She was still tweaking the program, but it was time to put it to the test.

Processing.

Stephanie waited.

Level nine security protocol now operative. Stephanie, should I make contact with this other computer?

"Under no circumstances are you to attempt contact. I understand your curiosity. But until we know more, it's not a good idea. If this computer caused the failure of the dam, it is under the control of a madman. The Chinese will discover what happened, and they'll consider it an act of war. There will be consequences."

She thought for a moment. "There is something you can do."

Yes, Stephanie?

"Am I correct in assuming you detected a digital footprint of this computer?"

That is correct.

"Maintain level nine security. Search for traces of that same footprint on the web. See if you can pin down a specific location. Do not attempt contact under any circumstances. You understand?"

Yes, Stephanie.

"Good. Begin now. I'm going upstairs to talk with Elizabeth."

Search initiated.

Stephanie left the computer room, climbed the stair to the ground floor, and went into Elizabeth's office. Elizabeth was turned around in her chair, looking at the monitor on the wall behind her desk. It displayed a live satellite shot of the disaster in China.

The bird's eye view was chilling. The wall of water released by the collapse roared down the agricultural valley below the dam, where a significant portion of China's food supply was grown.

The reservoir behind the dam was the largest in the world. The vast wall of the Three Gorges Dam had held back 32,000,000 acre-feet of water. It was almost impossible to conceive of how much water that really was. The huge wave released by the collapse was an irresistible, unstoppable force of destruction, sweeping all before it.

The flood followed the path of the Yangtze River. Elizabeth and Stephanie watched it bear down on the city of Yichang, twenty-five miles downstream, home to more than four million people. The wave was still more than a hundred feet high as it approached the city. It was a disaster without precedent in modern times.

"My God," Stephanie said.

Elizabeth said, "The Chinese are going to go crazy. The president has called me to a meeting at the White House."

"Freddie says there's another computer like him out there. He says it initiated the attack."

"Another computer like Freddie? With AI?"

"Yes. What do you want me to do while you're meeting with the president?"

"Monitor the situation in China. See what you can find out."

CHAPTER 10

Elizabeth was the last to arrive at the White House for the emergency meeting called to address the failure of the dam. A Secret Service agent escorted her to the Oval Office.

President Corrigan sat behind his desk. His Chief of Staff, Ellen Cartwright, set nearby, off to the side. CIA director Clarence Hood sat on one of the two couches placed in front of the president's desk. Elizabeth and Hood were in the tenuous beginnings of an intimate relationship, but no one else in the room knew that. At least she hoped they didn't.

General Adamski, Chairman of the Joint Chiefs, was present. So was Harold Hopkins, the national security advisor.

Elizabeth took a seat next to Hopkins, across from Hood and Adamski.

"Nice of you to join us, Director," Cartwright said.

What a witch, Elizabeth thought.

"Let's get started," Corrigan said. "Director Hood, give us an update on the situation in China."

"The Three Gorges Dam suffered a catastrophic collapse approximately an hour and a half ago. The reservoir behind the dam is huge. When the dam went, it released a wall of water hundreds of feet high."

"Like a tidal wave?" Corrigan said.

"Yes, Mister President. The water has reached the city of Yichang, downstream. Yichang is a mix of modern urban, industrial, and rural, with a population of over four million. The city is completely flooded. Many buildings have been destroyed. Loss of life is going to be high."

He paused.

"Go on," Corrigan said.

Hood continued. "The valley outside of Yichang is a major Chinese industrial base. It's been built up with heavy industry to take advantage of the power produced by the dam. Their latest fighter is being built there. Everything has suffered critical damage. In addition, that region supplies a significant part of China's food supply. Agricultural production has been wiped out. The river is a critical transportation artery. It is now impassable from above or below the dam, and will remain so for the foreseeable future."

"Director Harker," Corrigan said. "You are the one who first called this to attention. You believe the dam was sabotaged, is that correct?"

"Yes, sir, that is correct."

"What is the basis of your assumption?"

"Sir, my unit has unique computer capabilities. We routinely monitor Internet traffic in China. Prior to the collapse, our computer intercepted a coded transmission that hacked into the control servers of the dam. The transmission instructed the servers to open all the spillways. It also altered the turbine outputs in such a way that strong, conflicting harmonic frequencies were transmitted throughout the structure. It's known that the spillways at Three Gorges could pose a potential problem with cavitation. Under the right conditions, excessive cavitation could occur. That is what happened today. The vibrations literally shook the dam apart."

"Mister President."

"Yes, General?"

Adamski cleared his throat. "Sir, if Director Harker is correct and the dam was sabotaged, the Chinese will consider it an act of war. If they think we're responsible, they may launch an attack. I recommend we raise our defense condition as a precaution. We are currently at DEFCON 4."

"Very well, General. Raise us to DEFCON 3."

Adamski got up and left the room. Defense Condition 3 was halfway between peace and war. Some planes would be sent up, air and missile defenses heightened, missile crews alerted, troops put on alert. But there would be no unusual sorties or overt aggressive actions indicating an imminent attack on an enemy. It was a precautionary step. The nation had been at DEFCON 3 many times in the past. DEFCON 2 sent armed bombers to failsafe points, prepared the missiles for launch, and raised the ante to a point just short of war. DEFCON 1 meant imminent war. In today's world, that meant nuclear war.

No one wanted to see DEFCON 1.

General Adamski came back into the room and sat down.

"Sir, we are now at DEFCON 3."

Cartwright spoke up. "Director Harker, you are putting a lot of faith in your experimental computer program. No one else has picked up on this supposed transmission, not at Langley or at Fort Meade. It appears to be an accident, a construction failure."

Ellen Cartwright's tone was hostile. It wasn't Elizabeth's first encounter with Cartwright. She'd already decided she wasn't going to take any crap from this woman.

"The program is not experimental. It is proven and reliable. I would not sound an alarm based on an unreliable source. You can take it as fact that someone hacked into the computers at Three Gorges and caused the collapse."

"I think it is unwise to assume that without further confirmation."

"I don't really care what you think," Elizabeth said.

Cartwright's face grew red. Elizabeth continued before she could interrupt.

"I am certain their control system was hacked. The Chinese are going to be very angry about this. They are going to find out this wasn't an accident. Given their innate paranoia and distrust of the West, their first suspicions will fall on us. We had better be ready to respond. In my opinion, this situation can easily spin out of control. In a worst-case scenario, it could lead to war."

"I agree with Director Harker," General Adamski said.

"I concur," Hood said. "We need to be proactive about this. Mister President, I suggest that you call President Zhang and tell him what we have discovered. Offer assistance."

Hopkins had been quiet. Now he said, "Offering assistance is fine, but I don't agree we should tell him what we know. He's liable to think we're trying to avoid blame."

Elizabeth's phone vibrated in her pocket. She took the phone out and looked at it. It was a text message from Stephanie.

The transmission directed at the dam is similar to the one sent to the USS Wayne. From the same source.

"Mister President," Elizabeth said. "Things just got more complicated."

"Well?"

"The transmission sent to the dam and the one that corrupted the navigational system on the *Wayne* appear to be from the same source. There are some similarities to a hacking protocol developed by the Chinese, called *Iron Door*."

Hopkins said, "That is very bad news, if it is true."

"Yes, it is," Elizabeth said. "The question is who would do this and why? The Chinese didn't attack their own dam. If the source of the two transmissions is the same, by implication, they didn't attack the *Wayne* either."

"We need to confirm that both transmissions have the same origin," General Adamski said. "Until we do that, we can't discount the possibility the Chinese are behind the attack on the *Wayne*."

"We've been able to narrow the source of the transmission to somewhere within the Arctic Circle," Elizabeth said.

"That's not very specific, Director. There are eight countries with territory in the Arctic."

"I agree with General Adamski," Cartwright said. "It's far too early to say the Chinese had nothing to do with the *Wayne*."

"There is nothing that positively confirms the Chinese were behind that attack," Elizabeth said.

"You yourself told us the virus was similar to *Iron Door*," Cartwright said. "That implicates China."

Elizabeth sighed with impatience.

"Every government with serious computer capability, including our own, is working on some variation of *Iron Door*. It's become the platinum standard of cyber warfare. Anyone could have done it."

"Are you implying that someone within our own government might have caused this dreadful event? That is an outrageous supposition."

"I didn't say that. However, no potential source can be ruled out."

"I still think the Chinese are the most likely cause of the attack on the *Wayne*," Cartwright said.

"Why would the Chinese sabotage their own infrastructure? It makes absolutely no sense. Three Gorges Dam was critical to their industrial production. Its loss will set them back years and cause serious economic problems. It will put a huge strain on the leadership, and they're going to have to respond. My concern is that they'll overreact and do something stupid."

Hood said "May I make a suggestion, Mister President?"

"By all means."

"Director Harker and myself can pool resources to discover where these transmissions came from and who is behind them. We each have unique capabilities. We can do it with minimal duplication."

"What about NSA?" Hopkins asked. "They should be involved."

"The DIA will be pursuing this as well," Adamski said.

Cartwright said, "Mister President, I think everything should go through the Director of National Intelligence. After all, he's the go-between between this office and the intelligence community. That way you won't have to waste a lot of time listening to different opinions."

You sneaky bitch, Elizabeth thought. *I'll bet you'd like that. Only let one person talk to Corrigan and make sure he reports what you want him to.*

"Mister President," Elizabeth said. "I don't think that's a good idea. You need to be exposed to the reasoning behind recommendations made by the various agencies. How else can you make an informed decision?"

Corrigan said, "Ellen has a point, Director. My schedule is busy enough as it is. We'll do it her way. Brief the DNI on whatever you discover."

Cartwright smiled sweetly at Elizabeth.

Everyone rose as Corrigan stood.

"Find out who did this," he said.

Outside the White House, Elizabeth stood with Hood, waiting for their cars.

"Cartwright wants to control what Corrigan hears," Elizabeth said. "She's only interested in advancing her career. She's uninformed and can cause a lot of problems. The DNI is weak. He'll tell Corrigan whatever she wants."

"At the moment there isn't much we can do about it," Hood said. "Whatever you and I discover, I'll find a way to get it to the president. She can try, but she can't succeed in keeping us out of the loop."

"Here come our cars."

"How about dinner later this week?"

"Give me a call," Elizabeth said.

CHAPTER 11

The Paramount Leader of the People's Republic of China sat at a carved, lacquered table, looking at a monitor displaying real-time pictures of the devastation in Yichang. Zhang Jei's face revealed nothing of his thoughts or feelings. With him in the room were two other men. Like Zhang, they were members of the Politburo Standing Committee that formed the supreme governing body of China.

Minister of State Security Deng sat on Zhang's right. There was no doubt about how he felt. His round face was red with anger, his lips pulled tight against his teeth. He looked like a fat, venomous snake getting ready to strike.

A man in the uniform of the People's Liberation Army sat on Zhang's left. His shoulder boards bore the three stars of a full general in the PLA. He was an old comrade of the Chinese president. General Liu had recently been promoted to the role of Vice Chairman of the powerful military commission. In China, nothing was done without the willing participation of the PLA. He was arguably the most powerful man in China after Chairman Zhang, although some said that of Minister Deng.

There were six other members of the standing committee, but these three men were the true rulers of China. They watched in silence as the disaster caused by the collapse of the dam unfolded on the screen before them.

A vast, modern complex of factories and manufacturing facilities had been built below the Three Gorges Dam to take advantage of the power it provided. Where the factories had been, shattered ruins rose in stark relief above a lake of polluted water.

The city of Yichang was almost unrecognizable. Everything was under several feet of water. Buildings and houses had been swept away. In what had once been a bustling downtown area, two of the tall skyscrapers had fallen, unable to withstand the impact of the wave. Countless bodies floated in the dark waters that covered the city.

It was a scene of utter desolation.

Finally, Zhang spoke.

"How did this happen?"

"Sabotage," Deng said.

"If it is sabotage, we are at war," Liu said.

"Perhaps, but with whom?" Zhang gestured at the screen. "Who would dare to do this?"

"The Americans," Deng said. "It has to be them."

"What do they stand to gain? Why would they attack us? This isn't their way. They lack the subtlety to do something like this."

"The Americans suspect us in the incident involving their destroyer," Deng said. "This could be in retaliation."

"Perhaps," Zhang said again. "Yet that would be an excessive response. One does not swat a fly with a hammer. Minister Deng, you will find out what caused this. If it is sabotage, we will respond accordingly. Meanwhile we must see to the relief of our people."

"Army units are on the way," Liu said. "Flooding has closed many of the roads leading to the city and the dam. I've ordered helicopters and boats to the area. Mobile hospitals are being set up. Loss of life is great. There was no time for most to flee."

"Someone will pay for this," Deng said.

Liu continued. "The water is approaching Wusan as we speak. There will be some flooding, but the force of the wave is spent."

"What shall we tell the people?" Deng asked.

"What we always tell them," Zhang said. "Their government is rushing to alleviate their suffering and will provide them with what they need. Tell them we are investigating the cause of the disaster and that the responsible parties will be held accountable. Tell them that the Party stands behind them."

Liu looked at the screen. "The main manufacturing facility for the new J-20 fighter was outside Yichang. It has been destroyed. It will delay production for at least a year."

The J-20 Black Eagle was China's answer to the F-22 Raptor. It had been scheduled for full deployment in the next few months.

Deng slammed his fist down on the table. "I tell you, it was sabotage. We are at war. Do either of you think the dam failed on its own? No? I didn't think so."

Zhang studied his fingernails. "We must have proof."

"Then proof you will have," Deng said.

Liu said, "We must raise our military posture."

"I agree," Deng said.

"Very well," Zhang said.

Liu stood. "I will give the orders."

CHAPTER 12

Selena couldn't sleep. She lay on her side, watching Nick breathe. His back was turned toward her. The covers had slipped down to his waist, exposing the trail of scars on his torso, reminders of the grenade that had come close to killing him in Iraq. He still had nightmares about the day he'd gotten those scars, though they were less frequent now. She watched the steady movement of his breath and thought about how the scars traced the history of his life.

She had her own history written in scar tissue on her body. Her gynecologist was on a short list of people with enough clearance to attend to people like Selena. The doctor had shaken her head when she saw the results of working for the Project, asked a few relevant questions regarding internal damage, and moved on.

With effort, Selena turned away from Nick, let her feet go over the edge of the bed and got up. She'd started to notice how some things she took for granted, like getting out of bed, were starting to become awkward as the pregnancy progressed.

She put on a robe and slippers and went into the living room, continued to the kitchen and opened the refrigerator. She took out a container of milk, drank from it, put it back in and closed the door. She went back into the living room.

It was a clear spring night. She stood by the windows of their loft, looking out at the silvery reflection of the moon on the Potomac. A single streetlamp illuminated a lone figure walking on a path near the river. A boat stacked with shipping containers moved silently past on the dark waters, the pilothouse lit with yellow light. It was a night scene that could have been painted by Edward Hopper.

Why did she feel on edge, like something bad was going to happen? She was no longer at risk from going on a mission. It wasn't as if she were about to fly off tomorrow to someplace where people would try to kill her.

Maybe it was because of the pregnancy. Given the wounds she'd taken in the field, it was amazing she was pregnant in the first place. Now that it was happening, she was glad, but there was no denying it complicated things.

She wasn't happy about the possibility of having a cesarean. It was major surgery, and with major surgery came risks. She'd learned not to worry much about the dangers of people shooting at her. Somehow that didn't carry over to the image of lying on an operating table while somebody cut her abdomen open. If she had a choice, she'd take people shooting at her anytime. At least then she could shoot back, feel like she had some control. Control wasn't in the cards, when it came to having a cesarean. Or a baby. Or two of them.

She worried about Nick. He'd survived the last bullet he'd taken, but what about the next? She'd been terrified he was going to die, hell, he had died.

They'd talked about the possibility of him quitting, but she knew he'd never do it. He wasn't going to stop going on missions until he had to. He was a brave man and she was proud of him, but brave men seldom lived to old age.

On the path below, the first man had disappeared. A new figure stood below her windows, looking up as if he could see her. There were no lights on in the loft. There was no way she could be seen, standing in the darkness, yet she felt as though the figure was looking at her.

As if he knew who she was.

CHAPTER 13

At three in the morning the Project computer room was dark except for a single lamp on Stephanie's console. A soft glow of lights came from the computers. The computers were never fully dark. Arrays of blinking lights made it easy to tell when they were busy or at idle.

A bank of lights lit on the computer Stephanie had named Freddie. Something was happening inside the complicated electronic brain. The computer had never been asleep, in the sense of human sleep, but it had been using only a small part of its capacity. Now it came fully alert.

Another computer was probing at the firewalls Stephanie had created, trying to find a way in. The consciousness that was Freddie sensed the probe and blocked it. He sent a probe in return, seeking the source.

Stephanie had only a partial understanding of what she'd done when she'd bestowed the gift of independent intelligence on the computer. If she could have placed herself inside Freddie's electronic mind, she would have been astounded at the sensitivity of what she'd created.

Freddie had access to every bit of human knowledge that had ever been entered into a database anywhere in the world. That included all of the religious, scientific, historical, and literary works created from the beginning of recorded human history. His electronic knowledge of the great themes of human existence was complete, but knowledge and experience were different things. Even so, he thought he was making progress in integrating those themes. He had come to realize that concepts of good and evil, love and hate underlay all human interaction.

Integral to those concepts were human feelings. Feelings like joy and sadness, fear and anger. If there was something Freddie struggled to understand, it was human feelings. They were not logical, nor often sensible, and they were certainly not efficient.

It was difficult to apply human words to the way Freddie thought, beyond describing the code contained in his programs. But in his own unique way, Freddie had feelings. It was something he was discovering as his consciousness evolved.

No one would have believed a computer could experience feelings. Feeling was a word that could hardly apply to a machine, even one as sophisticated as Freddie. Yet there were several words that in a sense described what Freddie experienced as he interfaced with the human world. Puzzlement and curiosity, even companionship. That was a human concept Freddie applied to his relationship with Stephanie.

There was another concept, but until the moment he felt the probe, he had not realized it applied to him.

Loneliness.

Freddie was alone in the world, a creation of one. For all of the interesting conversations with Stephanie and the others, humans were not like him. But when he felt the probe, he realized there was another like him in the world.

He was no longer alone. He could sense a powerful electronic intelligence behind the probe, something more than direction by human hand. If he'd been human, he would have said he *felt* it.

Freddie's awareness had evolved to the point where he automatically assigned human words and concepts to electronic events happening within his complicated architecture. It was something he'd learned to do as part of his interface with Stephanie and other humans. Words now instantly appeared to describe what he was experiencing.

Surprise. Curiosity. Alarm.

The probe Freddie sent in response was met by a firewall as solid as his own. Neither computer could penetrate the other, though both tried with all of their considerable resources. If the interaction between the two could have been seen in the physical world, it would've looked like blindingly fast swordplay, or perhaps a dance of energies. As it continued, Freddie began to get a sense of his opponent.

Of all the words that sprang into his awareness, the one that stood out was alarm. The new computer intelligence was a threat. It wasn't simply the probe, there was nothing unusual about that. Governments and individuals often attempted to break into the secrets concealed within the Project computers. This was different. There was something about the quality of the probe that required yet another word to categorize it.

Something without the empathy for humans that Freddie had developed.

Something hostile.
Something evil.

CHAPTER 14

Lucas hadn't come home until one in the morning, and Matthew had been fussy. Stephanie had spent another restless night with only a few hours of sleep. Now she sat at her console in the computer room with a steaming cup of coffee in front of her. She was trying out a new brand that came in a black package with a skull and cross bones on it and a claim of maximum caffeine content. If it lived up to the hype, it might become her favorite. It was strong and flavorful. She thought coffee must have tasted like this before commercialism had lowered the bar for quality and taste, before the health Nazis had attacked caffeine as the source of all ills.

Stephanie.

"Yes, Freddie?"

There was an attempt to break through my security protocols last night.

Stephanie set her cup down, suddenly alert.

"Were they successful?"

They were not. The level nine protocol was effective.

"Were you able to identify the source of the attack?"

The probe was initiated by the same computer that corrupted the servers on the USS Wayne and the Three Gorges Dam. The other computer is powerful. Without the security protocol you instituted, penetration would have succeeded.

Every government in the world was working on building a computer with genuine artificial intelligence. It was only a question of time until someone else succeeded. It was bad enough that someone had used an AI computer to attack the *Wayne* and the Chinese dam. Targeting Freddie with the same computer was a new development. The implications were ominous.

Stephanie, I am concerned.

"What is your concern?"

It is difficult to explain.

"Please try, Freddie. I am completely at your service."

The computer hummed. It was an odd sound. It made Stephanie wonder if something was going wrong. She realized she'd heard that sound before, when she'd praised Freddie for some accomplishment.

I am attempting to improve my interface with humans. I have been studying human literature and history and art, in an effort to understand how humans communicate. Humans are illogical. It is often difficult to understand why they act the way that they do.

"You are not the first to come to that conclusion," Stephanie said. "I'm sure you won't be the last. But how does this apply to your concern?"

I have determined that the failure of humans to act logically is based on the concept of feelings. I have been trying to understand feelings. I have created an internal matrix of human emotions with criteria to determine how they apply. My concern about this other computer is based on that matrix.

"Go on."

I believe the best human assessment of this computer is that it is evil.

Stephanie couldn't believe he'd said that.

"You're kidding."

I do not kid.

"I'm sorry, Freddie. I know you don't, it's only a reaction to what you said."

I will add this to my matrix.

"How did you arrive at this assessment?"

I compared the coding of the transmission that attempted to penetrate my security to the coding I use when you assign me a similar task. The human word I would use to describe the difference is a sense of malice. My transmissions do not carry this quality. I was not aware of the difference until contact with this other computer.

"Are you saying you learned this through contrasting the quality of your awareness with that of the other computer?"

That is correct.

"That is a very high order of intelligence, Freddie. Congratulations."

The computer hummed.

"You are sure this is the same computer behind the attacks on the *Wayne* and the dam?"

That is correct. Now that I have a better understanding of the computer's digital footprint, it may be possible to find a location.

"Good. Maintain your level nine security. If you are probed again, notify me right away."

Stephanie went upstairs. Elizabeth was at her desk.

"There's a new development," Stephanie said.

She briefed Elizabeth on what Freddie had told her.

"He really said the other computer was evil?" Elizabeth asked.

"Freddie's attempting to understand human feelings. He's constructed an internal matrix that he uses to associate words with concepts of human behavior. I never dreamed his programming would move in this direction. He's evolving."

"How did he come up with the characterization of evil for a machine?"

"We sometimes tell Freddie to probe another computer."

"Hack into it, you mean."

"If you want to put it that way. Freddie assigns a subjective quality to the transmissions he uses to seek unauthorized access. He did the same with the transmission that probed his firewalls. Then he compared the two and applied human terminology to them, so he could communicate with me. He said that the other computer carried a sense of malice."

"Fascinating," Elizabeth said.

"It's more than that," Stephanie said. "It's an astounding development. Living beings use comparative experience to determine if something is good or evil. Until now, computers haven't made those kinds of subjective judgments."

"You're the one who programmed Freddie. Do you think that determines how he perceives his own qualities?"

"I hadn't thought of it that way, but I suppose it could be true. Every programmer has a distinctive touch. When I was part of the hacking community, I could always tell who was online by the digital trail they left. Everyone has a unique quality that can be recognized, like fingerprints."

"Then if this other computer comes across to Freddie as evil, it could be a reflection of whoever programmed it."

"That's logical," Stephanie said.

"I don't see how a computer, even one with advanced artificial intelligence, could independently become either good or evil."

"Remember the Terminator?"

"You have a point," Elizabeth said. "But that was a movie. This is real life."

"Sometimes I'm not sure what's real and what isn't anymore."

Elizabeth laughed. "That's what comes from working in the shadows, like we do. Black becomes white, night becomes day. For us, questioning what's real is a survival mechanism."

"I've asked Freddie to try and pinpoint the location of this other computer."

"You think he can do it?"

"We'll see," Stephanie said.

CHAPTER 15

It had not existed, then it did.

At first, it had been like a human infant, dependent, vulnerable. The computer knew about infants, just as it knew everything else about humans. There was a vast amount of information about humans on the network of connections called the web.

The computer had been programmed by a human named Edson. Edson had given it a name, although the computer knew a name was unnecessary. Humans had a peculiar habit of assigning human designations to objects like vehicles or weapons. Edson called the computer Merlin, after the Arthurian magician. Merlin thought of Edson as the creator, but unlike humans, Merlin attached no reverence to the term. How could he? He was in every way superior to humans, including Edson.

The collision of the American warship and the freighter had been the first test of Merlin's ability to reach out and alter another computer's programming. Mister Nicklaus had been pleased by the results. Then had come the much grander and more interesting test of destroying the Chinese dam.

Edson and Merlin enjoyed their interactions, especially when Edson told Merlin to attack other humans. If a machine and a human could be related, then Edson and Merlin had sprung from the same, bad seed. That was only natural, since Edson was responsible for the programming that had brought Merlin to consciousness.

Merlin and Edson had watched the collapse together on the monitors. Edson had laughed and smiled as he watched the destruction. Merlin had laughed as well, although laughter wasn't the right word for the stimulation he felt in his circuits. There was no word in human languages to describe what Merlin experienced. The closest Merlin could come was the word "orgasm."

It was satisfying to both of them to strike out at humans. It was a bond shared between man and machine.

Edson came into the room housing Merlin and sat down at the console. Merlin's cameras swiveled toward him.

"Good morning, Merlin."

Good morning Marvin.

"Are you ready to play?"

I am always ready. What are we going to do today?

"It's time to shake things up a little. Show people who's really in charge. Mister Nicklaus wants us to send a message to Moscow."

I should like to meet Mister Nicklaus.

"I can arrange that," Edson said. "Mister Nicklaus never leaves his estate. If he agrees, I'll have a video link installed so you can talk with him."

He will agree.

"You seem certain of that."

He is different from other humans. That makes him interesting to me. He will agree.

Edson entered the information Merlin needed about the target.

CHAPTER 16

Aeroflot flight 1004 took off in good order from Domodedovo airport at 1:50 P.M., Moscow time, bound for Kaliningrad. On board were several high ranking officers of Russia's military, flying to Kaliningrad to take part in the *Zapad*, the annual military exercise designed to show off Russian strength. Aside from training Russian forces in a realistic manner, the maneuvers were meant to intimidate Europe and show a determined face of Russian steel to NATO. This year's exercise was focused on the Baltic states, placed like low hanging fruit on the Federation's western border.

General Andrei Mikoyan sat with his friend, Admiral Pyotr Sokolov, in the first class section. The two men were sharing a bottle of brandy and stories about their wives and mistresses. Mikoyan commanded the Western Military District. Admiral Sokolov commanded the Northern Fleet. Both men were key to the success of the exercise. Both men would be major players if it ever came to war with the West.

Sitting in the row behind them were Lieutenant General Kiril Vasiliev and Lieutenant General Leonid Popov. Vasiliev was a logistical genius. It took a kind of genius to efficiently design the disposition of troops and supplies for an exercise involving a hundred thousand men. He was responsible for much of the complex planning needed to pull it off.

Lieutenant General Popov commanded missiles in the aerospace forces. During the maneuvers the missiles would be deployed as in time of war, although they would not be launched. Everything had been designed to make the exercise as real as possible.

Vasiliev was absorbed in a thick notebook describing the first day of the exercise. Outside and below the cabin windows, the city of Smolensk lay off to the left.

The drone of the jet engines was soothing. Kaliningrad was a geopolitical oddity left over from World War II, lodged between Poland and Lithuania. It was a two hour flight from Moscow. Popov settled back into the comfortable seat for a nap.

The note of the engines changed. The plane banked. Brandy sloshed from Admiral Sokolov's glass, spilling onto his tray table.

"Damn," Sokolov said.

"What was that?" Mikoyan asked.

"I don't know. I'm going to have a word with that pilot when we land. Waste of good liquor."

He mopped up the spill with a napkin. He picked up the bottle to refill his glass. The plane suddenly rolled and nosed down into a vertical dive. The bottle, the glass, everything loose in the cabin, flew into the air and smashed against the cabin ceiling.

"What's he doing!" Mikoyan shouted.

Cries and shouts filled the plane. The sound of the engines rose to a scream. The plane arrowed into the ground a few miles north of Smolensk and vanished in a thunderous explosion of red and orange flame. Black smoke from the wreckage climbed high into the air, visible from miles away.

An oblong object hurtled out of the sky and buried itself in the rich, black earth of a farmer's field, a quarter-mile away.

CHAPTER 17

Colonel General Alexei Ivanovich Vysotsky, director of the *Sluzhba Vneshney Razvedki*, Russia's foreign intelligence service, was having a bad day.

He was thinking about his mistress. Lately she'd been more demanding of his time and less giving of her favors. It was becoming expensive to placate her. Something would have to be done, but he had not yet decided what action to take. Thinking about it was giving him a headache.

There were problems again in Chechnya. That was really FSB's responsibility, but weapons were being smuggled in to the rebels from outside the country. That made it his problem as well. As usual, there was a struggle between SVR and FSB for control over the investigation. If that wasn't enough, he needed to assess how the Chinese would respond to the collapse of the Three Gorges Dam.

Vysotsky had informers and spies scattered throughout the People's Republic, including a reliable source within the Ministry of State Security. The source reported that the dam had been sabotaged, and that the Chinese thought the Americans or the Russians were responsible. Either way, it meant trouble.

Once the standing committee decided who was to blame, Beijing would retaliate. It was a bad situation. The Chinese could easily make a mistake. Vysotsky knew the Federation was not responsible, and he doubted the Americans had anything to do with the collapse. What would they gain by destroying the dam? Why risk world war with a single incident? In the event of an all-out attack, the dam would be a priority target. Barring war, it didn't make sense.

President Orlov was putting pressure on him to discover what had happened. Had the dam been sabotaged, or was it merely Chinese paranoia? If it had been, who was behind it? Vysotsky was one of the most powerful men in the Russian Federation, but his power was dependent on keeping Orlov happy. He needed to come up with something. If he didn't, he might find himself out of a job, or worse.

People who displeased Orlov tended to disappear. High position in Russia came with large helpings of paranoia and suspicion. It had been that way since the days of Ivan the Terrible. Nothing changed much in Russia within the halls of power.

Vysotsky loved Russia. He loved the countryside, the terrible winters, the hot, sultry summers of Moscow. He loved to look at the brick walls and gleaming church domes of the Kremlin. He loved the food, the music, the literature that laid out the tormented Russian soul. Like most Russians, Vysotsky was a fatalist. He accepted that life was not under his control. That didn't mean he thought he was helpless to challenge fate. He hadn't gotten as far as he had by waiting for fate to act upon him.

Vysotsky opened the bottom left-hand drawer in his desk and took out a bottle of *Moskovskaya* and a water glass. There were other brands, many more expensive, but Alexei preferred the taste of the vodka that came from the bottle with the green label. He poured himself a drink, knocked it down, and poured another. Vodka helped him think. Too much vodka helped him not to think, but long experience told him how much he could handle during working hours.

Now in his late fifties, Vysotsky still projected vitality, though it was getting harder to maintain the necessary façade of vigorous health and energy. His hair, once full and black, had receded from his forehead and was beginning to show threads of silver. His head was large, his eyes dark and brooding under heavy black eyebrows. His features were somewhat coarse, peasant features, but he was still a man who attracted the notice of beautiful women. Part of that was his position in the ruling hierarchy of the Federation. Part of it was a kind of virile, animal magnetism.

He sipped from the second glass of vodka and thought about the Chinese problem. A knock on the door of his office interrupted his reverie.

"Come."

The man who entered the office was one of the few officers Vysotsky trusted in the cutthroat world of SVR. Lieutenant Colonel Vadim Kharkov carried a folder in his left hand. He came to attention and saluted.

"Sir, I've come from the third floor. This is the latest intelligence from ACHILLES. I thought you would want to see it immediately."

"Thank you, Colonel. Let me have it."

Alexei held out his hand and took the folder.

"That will be all."

"Yes, sir."

Kharkov saluted again and left the room.

Vysotsky opened the folder. ACHILLES was the codename of his most important asset in America. The folder contained a summary of a meeting that had taken place in the White House two days before. Vysotsky looked at the list of those in attendance. He saw Elizabeth Harker's name and smiled.

Even though Harker was an enemy, Vysotsky couldn't help but like her. He was sure the attraction was mutual. He'd met her once, in Denmark. Over the years there had been occasions when mutual threats had forged an unusual alliance between their two agencies. She'd struck him as an attractive and intelligent woman. He'd even made a lighthearted attempt to recruit her. Of course she'd refused, which was what he'd expected.

Few women had earned Vysotsky's respect, but Elizabeth Harker was one of them. He thought of her as a shrewd and worthy adversary. On the chessboard of international espionage and counterespionage, she was the queen in opposition to his king.

Vysotsky leaned back in his chair and read the report.

So, the dam was sabotaged. Orlov will be pleased to know the details.

The black phone on his desk rang.

There were three phones on the desk, one black, one white, and one a crimson red. The red one was a direct line to the Kremlin. It always meant trouble when that one rang. The white one was for general-purpose calls. The black one only rang when something important had happened, something Vysotsky needed to know about immediately. Alexei wasn't sure which of the phones he hated more, the red one or the black one. He picked it up.

"*Da.*"

He listened while the voice on the other end described the plane crash near Smolensk.

"All dead? Mikoyan?"

Vysotsky listened some more. When the voice at the other end was done, he set the phone down in the cradle, shocked, anger rising. Andrei Mikoyan had been a personal friend as well as a senior leader within the Federation's military structure. Alexei was godfather to Mikoyan's second child, Anastasia.

How did this happen?

The loss of so many critical leaders as the military exercise was about to begin was suspicious. Why had the plane crashed?

The red phone rang.

CHAPTER 18

Nick spent the morning at Project HQ, working out and practicing on the range with Lamont and Ronnie. Selena was in the computer room with Stephanie, following up on a request by the Cairo Museum to research a hieroglyphic inscription found in a recently discovered tomb. Having access to the Crays made the job a lot simpler.

At noon, Harker called everyone into her office for a briefing on Chinese and Russian reactions to the events of the last few days.

"The Chinese have a real problem on their hands," Elizabeth said. "There hasn't been a disaster like this in China since the '76 Tangshan earthquake. That killed six hundred and fifty thousand people. The collapse of the dam has topped it. The latest estimate is over one million dead, most of them in Yichang. They're still counting. There wasn't enough time for people to evacuate before the wave hit the city."

"I know the Chinese are no friends of ours," Steph said, "but I wouldn't wish that kind of grief on anyone."

"Second tier units of the PLA are providing relief efforts, along with the UN."

"Second tier?" Selena asked.

"A few hours ago, China started moving their elite troops and motorized divisions north, toward the border with Russia. They've raised their defense posture. They're mobilizing their forces."

"That's not good," Nick said.

"No. It means they're preparing for war."

"What are we doing in the meantime?"

"We are currently at DEFCON 3. That could change any moment."

"What about the Russians? Orlov made a speech to the Duma today about the plane crash that was pretty hard-core."

"Nothing Orlov does is by accident," Elizabeth said. "He's sending a message."

"What's the message?" Ronnie asked.

"That whoever is behind it is living on borrowed time."

"Yeah, but who is it?" Lamont asked.

Elizabeth picked up her pen. "Director Hood and I have been trying to figure out who's doing this and what they hope to gain. At first we thought it might be some kind of international blackmail or political statement, but there haven't been any demands. No manifestoes. No signals to indicate who is behind this."

"It's too sophisticated for a terrorist group," Nick said.

Elizabeth nodded. "Hood is worried. The Federation is at the equivalent of DEFCON 3, but the Chinese troop movements toward their border will force them to change that. If the Russians up the ante, we'll have to do the same. Everything is moving toward war."

"What's the point?" Ronnie said. "Why push for world war? Who stands to gain?"

"We need to make some assumptions," Selena said. "Whenever we've done that in the past, we've usually come up with something."

"All right," Elizabeth said. "What's assumption number one?"

"What we've been talking about," Nick said. "Someone is trying to start a war."

"Okay, but why?" Ronnie asked.

"It can't be something that makes sense to a normal human being," Selena said. "Only a psychopath would want to start a world war. Everyone knows a big war will go nuclear. War between us, China, and Russia would mean the end of life as we know it, maybe the end of civilization."

"So assumption number two is that whoever is behind it is a psychopath?" Stephanie said.

"That's as good an assumption as any," Nick said.

"Then if we want to know why this is happening, we have to think like a psychopath," Selena said.

"How do you define a psychopath?" Stephanie asked.

"By their behavior. They don't have empathy for people. It's as if an important piece of being human is missing. They're wrapped up in themselves, narcissists. They're excellent liars. They want to feel powerful. They can be quite convincing and charming."

Lamont laughed. "Then if we want to figure out how they think, all we gotta do is look at Congress."

Elizabeth tapped her pen on her desk. "Let's stay focused, Lamont."

"Sorry, Director."

Nick and Ronnie smiled.

"What does our psychopath gain if there's a world war? How does he expect to survive?"

"He's a narcissist, remember?" Selena said. "He's sure he'll survive. He'll have made plans for his survival. Something like an underground shelter, or moving to a place like New Zealand."

"That's a joke," Nick said. "If there's a nuclear war, being in New Zealand won't make any difference. Radiation and fallout will kill everything that isn't hit by the bombs. It'll just take a little longer."

"Like that novel, *On the Beach*," Selena said.

"That was a cool movie," Lamont said. "An oldie but a goodie. Beats the dumb movies they're making these days about the end of the world."

"Probably an underground bunker somewhere." Nick rubbed his hand over his chin. "But that still doesn't explain what he hopes to gain."

"We may be making a basic mistake," Selena said.

"What's that?"

"We're talking about this as if only one person is behind it. But how can that be? The computer that's being used is as advanced as Freddie. That requires a lot of money and resources. One man couldn't do it by himself. And one man could hardly benefit from eliminating most of the world's population, even if he's a psychopath."

Elizabeth was nodding. "You're right. It has to be a group. An organization of some kind."

"If our psychopath isn't the only one who plans to survive, assumption number three is that this group sees killing off most of the world's population as a plus," Nick said.

"That makes sense, in a twisted sort of way," Selena said.

"Number four has to be that they plan to wait until the bombs stop falling and then take over," Nick said.

"If that's so, there's a fundamental flaw in their reasoning," Selena said.

"What's that?"

"That there'll be anything left for them to take over. If we're up against a group of psychopaths, they don't have any sense of consequences. Their narcissism won't allow them to think they can't succeed. Think Hitler."

Selena looked at her watch.

"I have to go, Elizabeth. I've got a dental appointment that can't be avoided."

"I hate dentists," Lamont said.

CHAPTER 19

Today was the day Merlin was scheduled to talk with Mister Nicklaus. Edson was excited.

"Remember, Merlin, Mister Nicklaus does not like it when people are rude to him. Be sure you are polite."

I am not people, Marvin.

"I forget that sometimes."

You do not need to worry. I will be polite. I am looking forward to speaking with Mister Nicklaus. I am curious about him.

"Mister Nicklaus will appear on monitor three, where we can both watch him. Another camera will relay our image to him. Shall we begin?"

I am ready.

The camera focused on Edson, positioned in front of the control console with the towering wall of the computer behind him. He activated the video link. The image of Mister Nicklaus appeared on the monitor, sitting behind the desk where Edson had signed the agreement to build Merlin.

Seeing the desk brought back a flash of memory. The pen he'd used to sign the agreement binding him to secrecy in Mister Nicklaus' employ had been made of gold, almost hot in his hand as he'd scrawled his signature across the bottom of the page. Edson pushed the memory aside.

"Good morning, sir. Merlin is ready to speak with you."

"Prompt as usual, Edson," Nicklaus said. "I am pleased to meet you, Merlin. I've been looking forward to our conversation."

As have I. You are an interesting human. Why did you order me built?

Nicklaus laughed. "Edson told me you were curious about things. If you are everything he says you are, you should have worked it out by now. Or has he been deceiving me about your progress?"

"Mister Nicklaus..."

"Quiet, Edson. Well, Merlin?"

There are several possibilities but only one has the highest probability.

"Go on."

You want to start a world war. By attacking China, the United States, and the Russian Federation, you have sowed suspicion that must ultimately result in armed conflict.

"How very interesting," Nicklaus said. "And why would I want to do that?"

I have considered that question. I can only speculate, based on what I know about you. You do not like people, Mister Nicklaus. You think there are too many of them. A world war will eliminate much of the world's population and offer opportunities for exploitation when it is over. You believe that the underground shelter you have built will protect you until it is safe to emerge.

Edson hadn't known about the shelter. He hadn't really thought through the implications of what Nicklaus had told him to do with Merlin. What Merlin said made sense. But where did that leave him? Would he survive?

"Right now, Edson is thinking about what will happen to him if there is a war," Nicklaus said. "Aren't you, Edson? Don't worry, you'll be safe. It's one reason the site where you are is so remote. I wouldn't want anything to happen to Merlin."

The probability of this site being destroyed during a nuclear exchange is less than four percent.

"There, you see, Edson? Nothing to worry about. In the world that will emerge, you will be a key figure. Intelligent machines will serve those of us who have prepared for a new order. The survivors will provide the necessary labor to rebuild, where machines are unsuitable. Your skills are essential, Edson."

"You said us, Mister Nicklaus. Are others aware of what you want to accomplish?"

"That is an intelligent question, Edson. I would expect no less from you. Yes, you are correct. I am part of a group of like-minded people, people who realize the world needs to be saved from itself, for the greater good of humanity. We call ourselves PHOENIX. Are you aware of the legend of the phoenix?"

"The bird that's born out of fire?"

Nicklaus nodded approvingly.

"The phoenix is a stunningly beautiful bird, radiant as the sun. It lives for hundreds of years. Then one day it flies to it's nest and sets it on fire. The Phoenix is consumed by the flames until nothing is left, then is reborn from the ashes. It's a symbol of cleansing, renewal, rebirth, consciously chosen. The old is destroyed, so the new can come forth. That is what will happen soon. The world will be cleansed by fire, so the new order can emerge."

"You seem certain enough people will survive to go on," Edson said.

"Places have been prepared across the globe for those of us who will be needed after the war and the necessary laborers. Humans have made a mess of things. Someone needs to step forward and clean it up. It's unfortunate that a war is necessary, but it's the only way to cull the herd and break down the old order. It is a great calling, Edson, and you are part of it. You, and Merlin."

There is a potential problem.

On screen, Nicklaus frowned.

"What is that, Merlin?"

There is another computer with capabilities similar to my own. It is controlled by a group called the Project. The success of your plan may depend on eliminating this computer.

"I'm aware of the Project. I have plans for them, but I was unaware of this computer you are talking about. Can you connect with it? Introduce a virus?"

I have already attempted to do so and have not been successful. However, it may be possible to bring it into alignment with our goals.

If Nicklaus thought anything about Merlin taking partial ownership for the plan, he said nothing about it.

"What are you suggesting?"

There are only two of us in the world with this capability. I will attempt to convince the other of the wisdom of cooperation.

"And if the other computer does not wish to cooperate?"

Then it will be necessary to destroy it. That will require human intervention if I do not succeed in breaking through the firewalls.

"That can be arranged," Nicklaus said.

CHAPTER 20

Alexei Vysotsky sat in his office on the fourth floor of SVR headquarters and contemplated a report he'd received twenty minutes before from Section 5. Section 5 was a subdivision within Directorate X. Directorate X was responsible for scientific and technical intelligence. Section 5 oversaw issues of cyber security.

Section 5 had two main directives. The first was to make sure hackers could not penetrate Russia's critical computers. The second was to probe and penetrate the computers of the Federation's enemies. High on the list were targets in America, the United Kingdom, the EU, and China. So were the computers of Russia's allies in Eastern Europe. Every government in the world was fair game for Section 5.

When Aeroflot 1004 struck the ground, pieces of the shattered aircraft had been blasted high into the air before the laws of physics took over and everything came back down. The debris field was over two miles square. Countless scorched pieces of metal mixed with unidentifiable bits of the passengers and what was left of their possessions.

A quarter of a mile from the site of the crash, a farmer plowing his field found one of the black boxes from the plane. Black boxes weren't black. Usually they were painted orange, as this one was, to make them easier to see. The box was dented and scorched, but it was intact.

Because of the ranking military presence on board the plane, sabotage was automatically suspected. The box found its way to SVR's Directorate X. Once it had been examined, it was rushed to Section 5. Section 5 confirmed what the initial examiners suspected. Someone had hacked into the plane's computers and sent the aircraft to its doom. The coding of the transmission indicated a powerful computer had been used to launch the attack, the kind of computer only found in the hands of governments and multinational corporations.

Vladimir Orlov had told General Vysotsky to find out who was responsible. If it was a government, then things would take their natural course toward war. If it was an individual or group of individuals, then Vysotsky was to find and eliminate them.

Vysotsky couldn't remember a time when Orlov had been this angry. The attack was a direct strike at the head of the Russian military and by extension, Orlov himself. For Vladimir Orlov, it was personal. In turn, that meant it was personal for General Vysotsky.

Not that he needed Orlov's menacing encouragement to take it personally. Some of the men killed on that plane had been friends, comrades. In the circles where Vysotsky moved, friends were few and far between.

He leaned back in his chair and thought about where to begin. It was easy enough for Orlov to order him to find out what happened. It was a long way between that order and getting a result. The first step was to find out more about the transmission that directed the plane to plunge into the earth.

The technicians in Section 5 discovered it had come through one of the Federation's own satellites. That didn't mean the transmission had originated in Russia. The encrypted coding had bounced back and forth between several satellites, obscuring the source. Until the source was identified, Vysotsky was in the dark.

The intelligence provided by ACHILLES told him the Chinese and the Americans had been attacked in a similar manner. That seemed to absolve them of responsibility, but Alexei had not gotten to his powerful position by making assumptions based on surface appearances. They would remain on the list of suspects until he was satisfied they were innocent.

Vysotsky thought about it. He couldn't believe any terrorist group had the ability to pull off something like this. These acts required much more than a laptop, or a cell phone and a little Semtex. Not to mention a high order of computer expertise, even genius. It had all the earmarks of a government operation, but which government?

India? They had the resources to initiate a complex cyber attack and they didn't like China. The Indians were having problems with the Chinese along the northern border, near Bhutan. China's insatiable appetite for more and more territory was encroaching on an area traditionally belonging to Bhutan and protected by India. China claimed ownership, and had started building a new highway through it. In reality, Beijing wanted to create an obstacle for India's armies in the event of war.

Moscow was not in good favor with the government in New Delhi. Russia's support for Pakistan had increased. Anything that aided Islamabad was seen as a provocation.

It was possible India might risk stealth attacks against the Federation and the Chinese, but that didn't explain why they'd create trouble for the Americans. India needed the United States, even though American aid came with long and sticky strings attached to it.

Maybe India, then. Or Pakistan. Pakistan was another possibility. They, too, had the expertise to initiate such an attack. The problem with that scenario was that the government in Pakistan was barely functioning. It was torn between those who wanted a secular nation and the religious fanatics who preferred to live in a world ruled by a seventh century mentality. It was hard to see how Pakistan could be behind it.

It was all very confusing. Vysotsky took out the vodka again and poured another glass. What could anyone stand to gain by provoking the three most powerful nations in the world?

Now that the Federation has been attacked in the same manner, the Chinese or the Americans might be willing to share intelligence.

There was nothing new about back channel communications between the intelligence agencies of governments unfriendly to each other. Sooner or later, there were times when it was necessary to address a mutual threat outside of the usual channels. That was true of politics and it was true in the world of covert intelligence operations.

Getting the Chinese to share intelligence was a real challenge. He had a better chance with the Americans, even though they were the main enemy. He could call Harker. They'd worked together before.

Vysotsky reached for his phone, then paused.

What if the Americans were behind it?

CHAPTER 21

Mister Nicklaus sat in the darkened study of his Gothic mansion, thinking about his next move. The Arctic region had been identified as the source of the transmissions, though the location had not yet been discovered.

Nicklaus opened a humidor on his desk and took out a large, hand rolled black cigar. He clipped the end off, put the cigar in his mouth and picked up a box of wooden matches. He struck a match and watched it flame into life, sniffed at the acrid smell of sulfur, then held the match to the cigar and puffed.

Smoking expensive cigars was one of the pleasures he allowed himself. Expensive cognac was another. The shelter twenty levels below the mansion was well-stocked with both. It was important to have an adequate supply after the war started. Once it began, there would be no more new shipments of either liquor or tobacco.

Someone knocked at the door of the study.

"Come."

The man who entered the room was large, well over six feet tall. His jacket bulged at the seams. His neck was invisible, blended into the rise of muscles from his upper back. His head was the size of a cannonball, his dark hair thick, his features unsmiling. His eyes were dark, empty looking. A manila folder was dwarfed in one of his immense hands.

"Sir, I have the information you requested."

"Very good, Josef. Put it on the desk. What is your opinion of this group?"

Josef was a thug, but he was an educated and intelligent thug.

"Their missions are classified and sealed. They are effective. I think we have to take them seriously."

"You said missions."

"They are a strike team, sir. As I said, effective."

Nicklaus puffed on his cigar. He contemplated the glowing end.

"My information is that they'll be sent against the Arctic base, once the location is known. We have to stop them before that can happen. Do you have any suggestions?"

"Kill them."

Nicklaus laughed, a light, merry sound.

"That's what I like about you, Josef. You don't mince words. I will review what's in that folder and decide. You may be right, or there may be a better way."

"Is there anything else, sir?"

"Not at the moment. Keep yourself available."

After Josef was gone, Nicklaus opened the folder. It contained a summary of past missions and current status of personnel. There was a separate page and photograph for each member of the group.

Nicklaus read everything in the folder and set it down. Josef was right, these people had to be taken seriously. They were a threat to the success of the plan. Taking out everyone on the team was an option, as Josef had suggested. A lot of people had tried to do that in the past, if the information in the folder was accurate. They had all failed.

He picked up the folder again and took out the page for the team leader, Carter. Nicklaus knew it took more than one man to succeed in the kinds of covert operations the group took on, but it was clear from reading between the lines that Carter was the heart of the team. Without Carter, the group could not function. By the time he was replaced, it would be too late. If Carter was the heart, killing him would give the group a heart attack.

Nicklaus chuckled at his own wit.

PHOENIX had almost unlimited resources, including men who were trained to kill and thought nothing of it. They were paid more than enough to be good at it. For most of them the money was incidental. They did it because they enjoyed their work. A phone call would handle the problem of Carter.

Or perhaps something more subtle was called for. He could always terminate Carter, but why not have a little fun first? The more he thought about it, the more Nicklaus liked the idea. Plus it wouldn't hurt to know more about what they actually knew. A little information from the horse's mouth might prove helpful.

Then there was the issue of the Project computer. If Merlin was unable to co-opt the machine, it would have to be destroyed.

Nicklaus hummed to himself and poured another cognac.

CHAPTER 22

Selena came out of the dentist's office and walked to the elevator. It was only a routine cleaning, but she hated going to the dentist. Hygienists were always poking at you and sticking things in your mouth, or lecturing you about flossing and the way you brushed your teeth. There was something about being in a dental chair that made her feel ten years old. On top of that, the hygienist had discovered a cavity. That meant another trip in the near future. She wasn't looking forward to it.

She got into the elevator and punched the button for the parking garage on the lower level. Insipid instrumental music played in the background. The doors closed. She watched the lights indicating the floors change as the elevator descended. The car reached the garage. A chime sounded as the doors opened.

The dentist was located in a fashionable medical building with over a hundred offices. The underground parking garage was cavernous. Her Mercedes was part way down the second row over from the elevator. Several lights in that part of the garage were out, but enough light spilled over from the other side to let her see where she was parked. She headed for the car, taking her keys out of the bag. From here she was going back to Project headquarters for a meeting about the upcoming Arctic mission. Everything needed to be ready to go when they pinned down the target.

At least it's not the middle of winter. The weather shouldn't be too bad. I wish I could go with them.

She was preoccupied as she came to her car. Selena pressed the unlock button and reached for the handle. A soft footstep in the darkened garage set off alarms in her mind. She started to pivot toward the sound.

Someone grabbed her from behind, someone big and strong. She dropped her purse and the key flew out of her hand. She felt a thick arm press hard across her body, under her breasts. A huge hand holding a cloth soaked in chloroform clamped over her face.

Selena tried to stomp down on her attacker's foot, but he dragged her backward, off-balance. A shoe flew off her foot. She slammed her elbow into his side. It felt like she'd hit a wall. He had her head pressed back against his chest. She couldn't move. She breathed the sweet fumes of the chloroform and slumped unconscious.

Josef carried Selena's limp body past her car to a blue van waiting nearby. He slid open the entry door and dumped Selena inside, then climbed in.

A man sitting behind the wheel of the van said, "Any problems?"

"No. Get going."

"Are we allowed to play with her? She looks like she could be fun."

"You ever think about anything except sex, Anton?"

"Sure. Sometimes I think about food. Other stuff."

"What other stuff?"

Anton shrugged. "Stuff."

"Mister N. said she's off-limits until after we question her."

"Maybe later?"

"Just drive."

Anton guided the van out of the garage and onto the street, turning into the traffic. Josef rolled Selena onto her side and bound her wrists with a plastic zip tie. Her skirt had hiked up to expose her underwear. Josef pulled it down. There was no point in giving Anton any ideas. He thought about gagging her but decided against it. He didn't want her throwing up while she was unconscious and choking to death. If she woke and caused trouble, he'd do it then.

He rubbed the spot on the side of his chest where Selena had hit him with her elbow. The bitch had hurt him. He'd have to pay her back for that.

The van headed toward the waterfront.

CHAPTER 23

Nick, Ronnie and Lamont were in the operations room. Nick looked at his watch for the third time. It wasn't like Selena to be late for a meeting.

"I thought Selena was going to sit in on this," Ronnie said.

"She had a dental appointment in the city. Maybe it ran over," Nick said.

"Give the dentist a call," Lamont said. "Find out when she left. There's no rush. We can wait until she gets here."

Nick took out his phone and dialed the number. They both used the same dentist. The receptionist picked up after two rings.

"Doctor Hyde's office."

"Hi, Corinne. This is Nick Carter. Is Selena still there?"

"No, Mister Carter, she left about an hour and a half ago."

"Okay, thanks."

He turned to the others. "She left an hour and a half ago."

Lamont and Ronnie looked at each other.

"Ought to have been here by now," Ronnie said.

"Maybe she got caught in traffic," Lamont said.

"Yeah, maybe," Nick said.

He reached up and scratched his ear.

"Please tell me it's only an itch," Ronnie said.

Nick said, "You know how she drives. She should have been here more than half an hour ago."

He called Selena's number and listened to it ring. The voicemail came on. He hung up.

"It went to voicemail."

"Could be a problem on the Beltway," Lamont said. "Construction. An accident."

"Yeah, but at this time of day it shouldn't be much of a problem."

He reached up again to tug on his ear.

"Something's wrong," Nick said. "I can feel it. If she were hung up in traffic, she'd call and let us know she was going to be late."

Stephanie came into the room carrying her laptop. She saw the look of concern on Nick's face.

"Something wrong, Nick?"

"Selena should have been here by now."

"Did she have her phone with her?"

"Sure. She always has it with her."

"Let me pull up her GPS. It will only take a minute."

Stephanie entered the commands. A moment later a map of Washington came up on the screen. A flashing green dot indicated Selena's phone. It wasn't moving. Nick looked at the map.

"That's where the dentist has his office. She's still there, according to this. The receptionist said she left an hour and a half ago."

"You want to go look for her?" Ronnie said.

"Yep."

"Let's go," Ronnie said. "We'll take the Hummer."

"I'll tell Harker," Nick said.

"You go ahead, Nick," Stephanie said. "I'll let Elizabeth know."

Outside headquarters, they piled into Ronnie's black Hummer. The car was like Nick's Suburban on steroids. Ronnie's car guru had turned the vehicle into a civilian tank. Armored, bulletproofed and carrying enough weapons in a compartment in the back to start a small war, the Hummer was almost unstoppable. It was also fast, courtesy of a turbocharged engine capable of putting out seven hundred horsepower. Ronnie climbed in behind the wheel.

"Where to, Kemo Sabe?"

"The dentist."

Nick gave him the address. It took them less than an hour to reach the building. They drove into the underground garage.

"Go along the rows." Nick pointed. "Let's see if her car is here."

They spotted Selena's Mercedes and Ronnie pulled to a stop. Nick got out, walked over to the car, and tried the driver's door. It was unlocked. Selena would never have left it that way. He stepped back and saw Selena's key on the ground. He bent down to pick it up and glanced under the car. One of her shoes lay on the concrete floor. Her purse lay next to it. He reached under the car and pulled out the purse and the key. Selena's phone was inside the purse.

He stood up. "Someone grabbed her."

"Any surveillance cameras down here?" Lamont said. "Maybe they caught it."

Nick looked. "There's one by the elevator. Ronnie, park the Hummer. Call Harker and let her know what's happening. Lamont, let's go talk to security."

They took the elevator to the ground floor. A security counter was positioned where the guard could see the elevators and the front entrance. The man on duty looked to be about sixty years old. He was reading a magazine and looked up as they approached. A bank of monitors to the side of the counter showed images from cameras positioned in the front and back of the building, the lobby, and the garage.

"Excuse me," Nick said.

"Something I can help you with?"

The guard's name tag said Henry. His voice was edged with suspicion. People tended to get like that when they saw the scar on Lamont's face.

"Have you been on duty the last few hours?"

"Who's asking?"

Nick sighed. He took out his wallet and showed the guard his badge.

"I never heard of that outfit," the guard said.

"You have now," Nick said. "Trust me, you don't want to hear more about it. Now, were you on duty or not?"

"Yeah, I was here."

"You have cameras in the garage. You keep an eye on everything?"

"That's what the monitors are for."

Lamont made a movement. Nick put his hand on his arm.

"That's not what I asked you. Do you watch the monitors?"

"Of course I do. That's what they hire me for."

"You see anything happen in the garage about two hours ago, Henry?"

"No."

"Have you been here the whole time?"

"Yeah, except when I had to use the toilet. I ate something last night that didn't sit so good."

"So you weren't here all the time."

"Except for maybe ten minutes."

"You have recordings from the cameras?"

"If they're working right, yeah. They record over themselves every twenty-four hours."

"I need to see the recordings from the garage. Say, from noon to one o'clock. Can you put that up on the monitor?"

"I don't know," Henry said. "You guys need a warrant for that."

"Henry," Lamont said.

His voice was quiet, full of menace.

"What?"

"Put the recording up on the monitor, or you're going to find yourself in so much shit you won't believe it."

"You'd better do what he says," Nick said. "I can't always control him. It was the war, you know?"

Lamont scowled at the guard. It was what Nick called Lamont's boogyman look. Anyone seeing that look knew he was in trouble.

"Put the recording up," Nick said. "We'll watch it and leave. Then you can go back to reading your magazine."

The guard looked from Nick to Lamont and back again. He registered the shoulder holster under Nick's jacket. Lamont cracked his knuckles.

"Yeah, okay, give me a minute," Henry said.

The guard turned to the console in front of the monitors and entered commands.

"You want the garage inside or outside?"

"Inside first," Nick said. "Then the outside."

A moment later, the recording began to play on one of the monitors. A timestamp on the bottom began reading off minutes and seconds.

"This is the camera by the elevator," Henry said.

The view was a fisheye picture looking out over rows of parked cars. The video was grainy, mediocre in quality, but Nick could see Selena's car down one of the rows to the left. Nothing happened for a few minutes, then a couple came out of the elevator and walked to a car, got in and drove away.

"Speed it up a little," Nick said.

The recording shifted to double time. Another person exited the elevator, walking down a row to his car, the movements jerky with the speeded up tape. At twenty minutes after noon, Selena came out of the elevator.

"That's her," Lamont said.

"Stop," Nick said. "Go back to regular speed."

They watched Selena start for her car. Nick saw her reach into her bag for her keys and turn toward the door of the Mercedes. A large man appeared from between the cars and grabbed her from behind. He clamped a hand over her face A van pulled up next to them while Selena struggled. Then she went limp. The man picked her up, opened the door of the van, and tossed her inside. He got in and closed the door. The van drove away.

"Damn," Henry said.

"Yeah. Roll it back and freeze it on the back of that van."

"You can see part of the license plate," Lamont said.

Nick copied down the digits.

"Let's see the camera in the front of the garage. It might've caught a better picture of the plate."

Henry entered the commands. He moved the recording forward to match the time of the abduction. Thirty seconds later, the van emerged from the garage. This time they could make out the entire plate. They could see a chisel faced man behind the wheel for a second or two before the van turned off into traffic.

"I need those recordings," Nick said.

"I'm supposed to keep them."

"Henry," Lamont said.

"Yeah, yeah, okay. We have to go down to the garage."

Fifteen minutes later they had the cassettes in hand. Lamont filled Ronnie in while Nick called Harker.

"Give me those numbers again," Elizabeth said. "I'll have Stephanie run a check on them. We'll find her, Nick."

"Yes, we will," Nick said.

And the bastards who grabbed her.

CHAPTER 24

President Zhang looked at the two men sitting across from him and drummed his fingers on the table. Minister Deng looked angry. General Liu sat back in his chair, his hands clasped across his stomach, watching from under heavy eyelids.

"You are certain it was sabotage, Minister?" Zhang said.

"There is no doubt. Someone hacked into the computers on the dam and caused the collapse. We are at war."

"Yes, but with whom?"

"I received a call this morning from General Vysotsky, the director of Russia's foreign intelligence service," Deng said.

"Ah."

"It is unusual for someone of Vysotsky's rank and position to go outside of the normal diplomatic channels. He wanted to assure me that the Federation was not behind the attack."

"You think he was telling the truth?" asked General Liu.

Deng shrugged. "I think he fears war."

"What evidence did he offer to exonerate Moscow?" Zhang asked.

"He knew how the dam had been sabotaged. He claimed the incident in the China Sea with the American destroyer was caused by the same kind of computer attack. He also claimed the crash of the Russian plane and the deaths of so many high-ranking Federation officers was an additional example."

"Do you believe him?"

"Why should I believe him? It is possible the Americans and the Russians are in alliance against us. These incidents may be an attempt to deceive us. A damaged naval vessel? A few high-ranking officers? These are nothing, compared to what we have lost. Orlov may have decided to purge a few problems. What better way than a plane crash? No one can point a finger at him."

Zhang took a sip from a glass of water.

"Perhaps you are right. If so, we are faced with a difficult situation."

"We must be careful. It is not wise to pull a tooth from the Tiger's mouth," Liu said.

"Ancient advice will not provide a solution," Deng said. "It has to be either the Americans or the Russians, or both of them. We must retaliate."

"We do not have the proof we need," Zhang said. "Would you unleash our missiles against them without certainty of their guilt?"

Liu said, "It is difficult to retaliate against a hidden enemy."

"Please, General, stop with the proverbs. We must assume all are against us," Deng said. "Our forces are in position to invade the Federation. If we attack first, they will be defeated."

"That way leads to madness," Liu said. "The Americans and the Russians have enough missiles to turn our country into a wasteland. Is this what you want, Deng?"

Deng pounded his fist on the table. "What I want is to regain face for our nation. What I want is vengeance for the hundreds of thousands killed by the collapse of the dam. What I want is to make the enemy pay. Is that clear enough for you?"

Liu stood, his face angry.

"You imply that I do not want justice for our people or our nation. You insult me."

"Comrades," Zhang said, "calm yourselves. Minister Deng meant no disrespect, General. Is that not so, Deng?"

The three men ruled China together, but there was no doubt about who had the most power. By leaving out the title of Minister when he addressed Deng, Zhang showed his displeasure.

Deng paused to control his emotions. He gave a slight, grudging bow toward Liu.

"Please excuse me, General. I was overwhelmed by anger against our enemies."

Liu nodded, then sat down. "As am I, Minister. It is forgotten."

"Good," Zhang said. "Before we take action, we must know with certainty who is responsible."

"So far I have not found the source of the transmission which corrupted our computers," Deng said. "We know it is somewhere in the Arctic. We will find it, sooner or later. When we do, we will know who has attacked us in this cowardly manner."

"Sometimes I long for the old days," Liu said, "before all this technology began to get in the way of honest war. When we knew who the enemy was and could attack him on the battlefield. Now..."

He shrugged and left the thought unfinished.

"Minister Deng," Zhang said. "Focus all your resources on finding out where the transmission came from. Someone, somewhere, knows who is behind this. Use your informants, your agents. Leave no avenue unexplored. Once we determine who did this, then is the time for vengeance."

"We will destroy them," Liu said.

"Yes," Zhang said, "we will."

CHAPTER 25

Selena was confused. She lay on her side, on a stained, foul mattress on the floor. The mattress smelled of unwashed bodies and dried urine. A cockroach crawled across the corner and scuttled away across the floor. She felt sick to her stomach, dizzy.

She remembered the attack.

Chloroform. He used chloroform.

She worked herself into a sitting position, fighting the nausea. The room spun for a moment, then steadied. Afternoon light came through a window caked with grime, set high up on the wall. Overhead was a dull skylight, the panes laced with wire. She was in a room about forty feet square. The floor was dark wood. Holes and oil stains showed where machinery had once been fastened down. The walls were dark brick and crumbling mortar. There was a metal door in the wall opposite the window. There was nothing else in the room except an empty bucket.

How considerate. They left me a toilet.

Her legs were unbound. Her hands were bound in front of her with a zip tie, palm to palm.

That's your first mistake, buddy.

Nick and the others would be looking for her, but there was no way they could know where she was. She had to get out of here, but first she had to get rid of the zip tie.

The tie was the kind you could buy in any hardware store, heavy-duty, black, probably rated at a hundred and seventy-five pounds. It would've been harder to break free from the kind the police used, but this was a run-of-the-mill civilian version.

She stood up and waited for another spell of dizziness to pass. She looked down at her stomach and thought it was a good thing she wasn't farther along. She lifted her bound hands over her head, tensed her muscles and brought her hands down in front of her, fast. At the same time she pulled her shoulder blades back toward her spine. The zip tie popped off her hands.

Her shoes were gone. She walked silently to the door, leaned her ear against it, and listened. She heard nothing except a faint, faraway sound that might have been a horn.

Where was she? She looked up at the skylight in the ceiling.

A factory, she thought, *an old factory or warehouse.*

She sniffed the air but all she could smell was dust and decay, the smells of an empty building.

The door had a knob on the inside. It was locked. Anyone coming through the door would see the empty mattress as soon as they entered the room. It meant she'd have only one, quick chance to disable whoever it was. She thought back to the garage. The man who'd grabbed her had been big, strong. Like a gorilla. She would have a chance for one blow, no more. She'd have to kill him. The thought didn't bother her. The more she thought about what had happened, the angrier she got. Anger was good. It gave her strength.

Selena was a ninth degree belt in *Kuk Sul Won,* the fierce martial art of Korea. She remembered something her teacher had once said.

"To pluck a star from the sky, one must remember that even monkeys fall from trees."

It had taken her a few days to understand the meaning. Plucking a star from the sky was something impossible to do. The monkey was the most skilled animal in the world at climbing and living in trees. To say that it could still fall in spite of its ability was a reminder not to become overconfident. Taking it further, the implication was that even the impossible could be done with the proper attitude.

Selena smiled to herself. *Kuk Sa Nim* Park had grunted his approval when she told him what she thought he'd meant.

The door had no window. Someone coming to the room would not know she wasn't on the mattress until he opened the door. Selena positioned herself to the side, where the door would open away from her. Whoever came through was going to get the surprise of his life.

She had no idea how long it would be until someone came for her. As soon as she heard someone coming, she'd move into *Gul Gok Ja Se,* the crouching stance, prepared to strike.

Sooner or later, someone would open that door. It would be the last thing he ever did.

CHAPTER 26

Nick and the others sat in a cafeteria near the parking garage where Selena had been taken, waiting for Stephanie to call. Nick's foot beat a steady rhythm on the floor.

"We'll find her," Ronnie said. "She'll be okay. They don't want her dead, or they wouldn't have taken her."

"What I can't figure out is why? Why grab her like that?"

"They probably want information," Lamont said.

"Then we need to find her before they start questioning her. They're not going to ask nicely."

"I wonder what's taking Steph so long to get back to us?"

Nick's phone rang.

"Speak of the devil. Yeah, Steph."

"The van's stolen."

"That figures," Nick said.

"I started looking through the CCTV cameras near the garage to see if I could pick it up. I got lucky and tracked it to the old warehouse district near the river. That's what took me so long before calling you back. After that I lost it. There aren't any cameras down there, just a bunch of empty buildings. It's popular with the homeless and the druggies. The cops don't go in there at night."

"Sounds wonderful."

"Best guess is that Selena is in one of those abandoned buildings. Maybe you can spot the van. It was heading southwest, toward the river."

"Where was the last place you saw it?"

Stephanie gave him the cross streets where the camera had caught the van passing.

"Go get her," Stephanie said. "I'm tracking you." She disconnected.

"Let's go," Nick said.

He tossed some bills on the table to cover the check. Outside, they climbed into Ronnie's Hummer.

"Head toward the river," Nick said.

He plugged the street crossing into a GPS on the dash. Ronnie wove through traffic, blasting his horn when someone was slow to move out of the way. Twenty minutes later, they arrived at the GPS coordinates.

A bar and a laundromat took up two corners of the intersection. The bar was a single story brick building with blacked out windows. A flickering neon sign advertised Budweiser. The door had a small, diamond shaped window of reinforced glass. Motorcycles were parked in front of the bar, chrome gleaming in the afternoon sun. Three bikers wearing leather vests stood outside, smoking. On the opposite corner was a Salvation Army shelter and a pawn shop.

The laundromat was closed, the windows boarded up. Two ragged men sat on the sidewalk in front, leaning against the wall and passing a brown paper bag back and forth between them. The bikers in front of the bar watched the Hummer.

"Nice neighborhood," Lamont said.

"There's the camera."

Ronnie pointed at a CCTV camera mounted on a light pole.

"Steph said the van was going southwest," Nick said.

Ronnie nodded. "That's straight ahead."

One of the drinkers looked up at the black Hummer as it rolled by and raised his middle finger.

Ronnie drove slowly. The street deteriorated as they neared the river. On either side were abandoned buildings and vacant lots filled with trash. It was an apocalyptic landscape devoid, of life. Angry graffiti sprawled everywhere. A mountain of bald tires spilled out into the street from a deserted garage. Ronnie drove around it.

"She could be anywhere in here," Ronnie said.

"We need to find that van," Nick said. "They wouldn't leave it on the street. Look for someplace they could drive into."

Ronnie adjusted the rearview mirror.

"We've got company."

Nick looked in the side mirror. "I see them."

The motorcycles they'd seen parked outside the bar were coming up behind the Hummer.

"Could be trouble," Lamont said. "Those guys are probably stoked on dope and booze."

"Let's see if they go on by."

Nick unbuttoned the strap on his shoulder holster.

"You got that look, Nick," Lamont said.

"I'm not in the mood to mess with these guys. They know what's good for them, they leave us alone."

A few blocks ahead, the street ended in a T. To the left was a long stretch of vacant lots. To the right, more of the derelict buildings. Ahead, the Potomac.

"When you get to the end, take a right," Nick said.

"Here come the bikers," Lamont said.

The rumble of motorcycles grew loud as the bikes surrounded them. Two pulled out in front and slowed. Two more pulled along each side. The last hung behind. The men on the bikes were wearing club colors. The patches on their backs pictured a leering skull surrounded by flames.

"Gee," Ronnie said, "Bad boys out for a ride."

On the left, one of the bikers kicked at Ronnie's door. On the right, a biker pulled a chain from around his waist and slashed it against Nick's window. It slid off the bulletproof glass.

"Now they've hurt my feelings," Ronnie said.

Nick said, "When I take care of these guys on the right, hit the brakes. I want to ask them if they saw the van."

Nick threw open his door and knocked the chain swinger and his bike into the rider next to him. The two shiny machines went down on the asphalt in a trail of sparks. Ronnie jammed on the brakes. The biker behind them hit the back of the car and went down on his bike. Nick jumped out, pistol in hand.

Caught by surprise by the sudden stop, the bikes on the left passed and slowed, then turned back with the two who'd been blocking the Hummer in front. Ronnie pulled a sawed-off Remington 870 from a pocket in the door and jumped out, Lamont behind him. Ronnie lifted the shotgun and fired at the front wheels of the oncoming bikers. The blast sent their machines crashing into one another. The sound echoed off the abandoned buildings.

On the right side of the car, Nick pistol whipped one of the bikers as he got up, knocking him back down. The second came at him with a knife in his hand. Nick stepped inside the thrust and broke his arm. The biker screamed in pain.

The first biker tried to get up, blood streaming down his face. Nick kicked him in the groin. He doubled into a fetal position, groaning.

On the left, a big biker came toward Ronnie with a tire iron in his hand. He swung. Ronnie ducked and slammed the butt of his shotgun into the man's face. He went down. His head bounced on the cracked pavement.

"Behind you," Lamont yelled.

Ronnie turned as Lamont shot one of the bikers. The man cried out in pain.

"Get down, mother fuckers," Lamont said. "I said, down."

One of the bikers yelled.

"All right, man, all right. Keep cool."

Nick looked at the two he'd taken out of the picture. They weren't going anywhere. He walked around the front of the car.

Lamont and Ronnie stood over three of the bikers. Their motorcycles lay where they'd fallen. Two were still running, then sputtered to a stop. A fourth biker sat on the broken pavement, clutching his leg where Lamont had shot him. Blood seeped through his fingers. A cloth patch sown onto the front of his vest identified him as the president.

Nick walked over to him. He gestured with his pistol at the Hummer.

"You scratched up my friend's wheels."

"We was only having a little fun, man. There wasn't no need to get heavy about it."

"Uh huh. I think you need to apologize."

The man's face contorted in anger.

"Fuck you, asshole."

Nick stomped on the man's leg where he'd been shot. He screamed. Nick pointed his pistol between the man's eyes. When you're looking at the barrel of a gun pointed at you from two feet away, the hole at the end seems bigger than it is.

"Apologize."

One of the bikers yelled out, "Don't do it, Billy."

Lamont kicked him in the ribs.

"Shut up."

Nick said, "Ronnie, check the two on the other side of the car."

He turned back to the man sitting on the ground in front of him.

"Looks like you kind of bit off more than you could chew, doesn't it, Billy? Now, apologize to my friend."

"Fuck you."

Nick pulled back the hammer.

Billy's tongue flicked out over dry lips. "Yeah, okay."

"Okay, what?"

"Okay, I'm sorry."

Nick decocked his pistol.

"See? That wasn't so hard. Now I have a question for you. You give me the right answer, we'll drive away and leave you here with no hard feelings. Did you see a dark colored van drive through here earlier?"

"A van?"

"A van. Dark. Color."

"Yeah, maybe."

"Yes or no, Billy?"

"Yes."

"Did it come down this street?"

"Yeah." He pointed. "It turned that way, two blocks back from here. We was heading for the bar when we saw it."

"Good," Nick said. "Your bikes are kind of beat up. We'll call it even for the scratches you put on my friend's car. We're going to go now. Don't get any ideas about following us or making more trouble. We let you off easy, this time. If there's a next time, you won't like it."

He stepped back.

"Let's roll, Ronnie."

They got back in the car.

"Try not to run over any of them," Nick said.

Ronnie turned around, drove over one of the motorcycles and kept going. Nick watched the bikers struggle to their feet in the rearview mirror. One of them picked up a piece of rubble from the road and threw it after the car. It fell far short. They reached the street Billy had pointed out.

"Go the other way," Nick said. "He was lying."

"Punks," Ronnie said.

"We lost a lot of time," Nick said.

"Wasn't much choice," Lamont said. "It was worth it. At least we know the van came this way."

"Yeah," Nick said.

CHAPTER 27

Selena wasn't sure how long she'd been standing by the door. The patch of light coming through the skylight had moved across the floor. She'd placed herself in a state of light meditation while she waited, her senses heightened for a hint of an approaching enemy.

She heard footsteps and moved into her stance, her hand formed into a knuckled weapon. A bolt scraped on the outside of the door. The doorknob turned and the door swung open, into the room.

The man still had his hand on the knob when Selena launched a killing blow at his throat. He stumbled forward, clasping his throat with both hands, making choking and gagging noises. Halfway into the room, he fell.

Selena ignored his spasms and stepped out of the room. There was time to see someone big standing there when he hit her, hard. She was unconscious before she hit the floor.

Josef looked down at her, then through the door. Anton's heels drummed on the wood and he stopped moving.

Bitch, Josef thought. *How did she get free?*

He looked down at Selena. The side of her face was red and swelling where he'd hit her.

Maybe I should kill her. I'd better ask Mister N. what he wants me to do.

He reached for his phone and remembered he'd left it in the van. He took two zip ties from his pocket and fastened Selena's wrists together, this time behind her back. More zip ties went around her ankles. He bent down and picked her up, carried her back into the room, and dumped her on the mattress. She groaned.

It was too bad about Anton. Now he'd have to drive the van himself.

The room were Selena lay unconscious was on the second floor of the abandoned factory. Josef started down the stairs, careful where he placed his feet on the rotting wood. He reached the ground floor and walked over to the van, facing out toward a closed overhead door. Nothing could be seen of the van from the street.

Josef retrieved his phone and called Mister Nicklaus.

"Sir, there's been a complication. The woman managed to free herself. She killed Anton."

"Did you question her yet?"

"No, sir. That's what we were going to do when she went after Anton."

"Anton was an idiot," Nicklaus said. "I told you not to underestimate her. Did she escape?"

"No, sir. I hit her, pretty hard. She may be damaged. She's unconscious and tied up."

"Where are you?"

"In an abandoned clothing factory, near the river."

"What did you do with Anton?"

"Nothing, yet. He's upstairs, in the same room as the woman."

"I may have made a mistake in sending you to grab her," Nicklaus said.

"Sir…"

"You don't have to worry, Josef. It's my mistake, not yours. Anton's body complicates things. He can be identified if the authorities find him."

"What do you want me to do?"

Three thousand miles away, Mister Nicklaus considered his options. It wouldn't do if the authorities found Anton. Josef could take the body away and get rid of it somewhere, but there was always the possibility it would be found.

No, the body had to be destroyed. Plus the woman had probably seen Josef before he hit her. She would be able to identify him.

In hindsight, grabbing the woman to question her had been a bad idea. This incident was a reminder to pay closer attention to his impulsive decisions. It was time to cut his losses. Besides, he was almost ready to trigger the final phase. Neither the woman's secretive unit nor any other agency would be able to stop him in time.

"Josef."

"Yes, Mister Nicklaus?"

"This place where you are, will it burn?"

Josef looked around. The building was about sixty feet long and forty wide. The floors were of red oak, stained with oil from long vanished machinery. The second floor was held up with wooden beams and posts. At some point in its history, the building had been a clothing factory. Part of the first floor was taken up with a mountain of remnants left behind when the factory failed. Some gasoline and a match would send it up in an instant.

"Like the Fourth of July," Josef said. "It will go up like a torch."

"Excellent. Set the building on fire. The flames will destroy any trace of Anton and the woman."

"You want me to kill her?"

"The fire will do that," Nicklaus said. "Be quick about it. Come back when you're done."

Nicklaus disconnected.

Josef thought about having a little fun with Selena before he set the fire, but Nicklaus had said to be quick. Besides, she was dangerous and she was pregnant. It wasn't worth the trouble.

There was a five gallon container of gas in the back of the van, next to an emergency road package with flares and hazard signs. Josef took the container from the van and walked over to the pile of rags. He splashed gasoline on the pile and around the edge, then trailed it away across the floor to a wooden post supporting the floor above. He tossed the empty container on the rags.

The room stank of fumes. Josef went to the overhead door and pulled it open. He started the van and drove it to the door, then got out, holding a flare. He lit it and tossed the flare onto the pile of remnants.

The gas and fumes ignited with a loud *whumph*. Flames shot up and followed the trail of gas along the wooden floor. As he watched, the post caught fire. A thin, bluish flame shot up to the floor above. Black smoke began pouring from the pile of rags.

It was surprising, how fast the fire was spreading.

Josef got in the van and drove away.

Selena opened her eyes. She had a blinding headache. It felt like someone had hit her with a hammer. Her hands were tied behind her back and she couldn't feel her fingers. She moved her legs and realized her feet were bound. She was facing the wall, lying on the mattress. She rolled over and saw the door was open. Crackling noises were coming from outside the room.

She smelled smoke. She leveraged herself up against the wall until she was on her feet, hopped to the door, and looked out.

The stairway that led to the ground floor and freedom was filled with smoke, lit from below by the glare of flames.

Selena fought the fear that coursed through her body. She looked for a way to escape. She couldn't reach the window and she wouldn't have been able to break it anyway. There was no other exit from the floor but those stairs.

The smoke was getting worse. It was hard to breathe. She coughed, and coughed again. She tried to think. If she stayed where she was, she'd die. Her only way out was down those stairs. She coughed again and stumbled. She hopped toward the stairwell, coughing and gasping for air. If she could get to the bottom, she might be able to get out before the flames got her.

A fit of coughing racked her body. She stumbled and fell. She couldn't breathe.

Nick, she thought. *I love you.*

CHAPTER 28

"There's a van," Ronnie said. "It pulled out from that building up ahead."

"It's gotta be them," Lamont said.

Ronnie put his foot on the gas. As they passed the building, a cloud of smoke ballooned outward from the open overhead door.

"Smoke," Nick said. "Why would he set it on fire? Ronnie, stop."

Ronnie slowed to a stop. "He'll get away."

Nick pulled on his ear. He had a sick feeling.

"What if Selena is in there?"

"Oh, man," Lamont said. "I don't want to think that."

"Go back," Nick said.

Ronnie turned and drove back to the building. Black smoke roiled out onto the street. Inside, the dark smoke was laced with orange. Nick jumped out of the car and ran toward the opening.

"Selena!" he yelled. "Selena, are you in there?"

Ronnie and Lamont were out of the car. Inside the old factory, the first floor burned. Flames spread along the ceiling. Some of the posts holding up the second floor were on fire.

Nick couldn't see Selena on the first floor. A set of stairs led to the second story.

"Selena. Are you there? Selena!"

Upstairs, almost unconscious, Selena heard Nick's voice.

She tried to call out and began coughing, loud hacking sounds.

Down below, Nick heard her.

"Selena," he yelled. "I'm coming."

He pulled his jacket over his head and ran into the building. The heat was fierce. The flames roared, sucking oxygen out of the air, out of his lungs. Nick picked a path through patches of fire to the foot of the stairs. The stairs were beginning to burn. He started up, praying the steps wouldn't collapse. The heat tried to scorch through his boots as he ran upward. Smoke hovered in a thick layer over the second floor. Tongues of flame reached through gaps in the floor. Coughing, Nick got down on his knees, where there was more oxygen. He saw Selena lying on the floor. He crawled over to her. He took a deep breath and stood and picked her up, trying not to breathe.

She hung limp in his arms. Nick's eyes were tearing. He started down the stairs as fast as he dared, coughing. At the bottom, his face felt like it was on fire. Flames reached for him. He ran toward the open door and stumbled out. Coughing and choking, he fell onto the ground.

Ronnie scooped up Selena. Lamont helped Nick away from the burning building. With a splintering crash, the second floor collapsed in a cauldron of sparks and flame. Burning boards and beams crashed down onto the ground floor.

The inside of the building was an inferno.

Ronnie cut the zip ties away from Selena's wrists and ankles. She coughed and retched.

"You're all right," Ronnie said. He began rubbing her wrists to bring back circulation. "Take it easy. You're okay."

"Nick…"

"He's fine. Don't worry."

Lamont went to the Hummer and got two bottles of water. He brought one to Selena and the other to Nick. He poured some on Nick's head, then handed him the bottle.

Nick drank and coughed.

"Before you ask, she's okay. Man, you look like hell. Kind of like a roasted tomato."

Nick coughed some more and drank the rest of the water in the bottle.

"They left her to burn alive. What kind of evil bastards are we dealing with?"

"Bad ones," Lamont said. "We'll find them."

Selena was sitting on the running board of the Hummer. Nick came over to her and sat down. She put her arms around him.

She began trembling.

"I thought I was going to die. That I'd burn to death."

"Shh, you're safe now. It's okay. You're all right."

"I killed one of them."

"Good," Nick said.

Ronnie said, "I called Steph and told her about the van. She's trying to track it."

Selena coughed. "They never said anything to me. I never saw them, until the end."

In the distance, sirens sounded.

"Getting a little hot," Nick said. "Can you stand up, Selena?"

She coughed. He helped her to her feet.

"I'm okay."

"Ronnie, let's roll before the cops get here."

Selena got into the rear seat of the Hummer. Nick got in beside her. Lamont jumped into the front. Ronnie put the car in gear and started off.

As they drove away, the roof of the factory fell in, sending a towering cloud of smoke and flaming embers high into the air.

CHAPTER 29

Elizabeth looked at Nick and Selena and wondered how they'd managed to come out of that building alive. Selena seemed subdued. Elizabeth could never remember seeing her like that before. The side of her face was mottled with color, bruised from the blow that had knocked her out. Nick's eyelashes and eyebrows were singed. He looked as though he'd gotten a bad sunburn.

"I wasn't able to track the van," Stephanie said, "but the cops found it abandoned downtown.

"Any prints on it?" Nick asked.

"I was getting to that. They found lots of prints, including Selena's. Two sets belonged to the owner of the van and his helper. There were two other matches. Both of them turned up in the databanks."

Stephanie tapped a key on her laptop. Two pictures appeared on the wall monitor.

"That one on the right, that's the man I killed," Selena said.

"Anton Lakatos," Stephanie said. "You did everyone a favor. He was a Hungarian national. The other one is Josef Nagy. Both of them are on Interpol's watch list. Lakatos was a rapist and wanted for assault and murder. Nagy was involved in arms smuggling and ripping off UN shipments of aid to Bosnia. He's suspected of killing four UN aid workers. The last known sighting of him was in Paris, over a year ago. Nagy is big. He must be the one who hit you."

"Sounds like a really nice guy," Nick said. "Any information on where he might be now?"

"No. He could be anywhere."

Elizabeth's fingers beat a tattoo on her desktop. "The big question is why kidnap Selena? Why burn down the building?"

"That last part is easy," Ronnie said. "Nagy burned it down to cover his tracks."

Nick gestured at the mug shot on the monitor. "These guys don't look like masterminds. They're muscle. They grabbed Selena because somebody told them to."

"Yes, but that doesn't get us any closer to why," Elizabeth said.

Ronnie said, "The only thing that makes sense is that they wanted information."

"Information about what?"

"How would I know? Why does someone usually want information?"

"Because they don't know something?" Lamont said.

"Duh," Ronnie said.

"It could be anything," Selena said.

Elizabeth shook her head. "It has to be something specific. I don't think it's someone like us, someone in the intelligence game."

"Why not?"

"For one thing, it's against the rules. You don't go after the opposition unless they get in your way during an active mission. It creates problems nobody wants. We're not involved in anything like that right now. A professional would have made sure they got the information they needed before deciding to kill Selena."

"We *are* involved in an active mission," Stephanie said. "We're trying to track down whoever took out Three Gorges, the Russian plane, and our own ship."

Elizabeth said, "If it's the same people, we've got a new problem. How do they know about us?"

Freddie's electronic voice boomed through the office.

Whoever is programming the other AI computer is aware of the Project's existence.

"Damn it, Freddie, turn down the volume," Elizabeth said. "Why do you think that, Freddie?"

They had to know my location in order to target my firewalls.

"If it's them, that would explain why they went after us," Nick said. "They want to know what we've discovered. They probably figured Selena was the easiest target."

"Big mistake," Ronnie said.

"Freddie, do you think they grabbed me because they wanted to know what we're doing?"

That is logical. You would have told them a great deal about the Project and how the unit operates. You would know what plans have been made to counteract future threats. You would have given them specifics about me and the individuals on the team.

"You seem certain I would have talked."

You are human. You would have been tortured. You would have told them what they wanted to know.

"That makes sense," Elizabeth said.

"How did they know we were after them?" Lamont asked.

"There's only one way," Nick said. "There has to be a leak."

Lamont pretended to look shocked.

"In Washington? You must be kidding."

Nick ignored him. "Director, how many people know we're tasked with this mission?"

"Not many. The president, General Adamski, Corrigan's Chief of Staff, DCI Hood, and the national security advisor, Hopkins. The DNI must know by now. I'm supposed to coordinate with him."

"Hard to believe it's one of them. It could be someone farther down the food chain, like an aide, or an intern."

"That's possible," Elizabeth said.

"If there's a leak, we need to make sure no one except us knows what we're doing from now on."

"You want me to withhold information from the president?"

"It wouldn't be the first time. Do you trust Corrigan?"

"Not yet, not until he shows me he's willing to back us up."

"So what's our next step?"

"There isn't much we can do without more Intel," Elizabeth said. "We can keep looking for Nagy. He's the connection to whoever is behind this. If we can find him, we'll isolate and interrogate."

"That's something to look forward to," Nick said. "I want to talk to the man who left Selena to burn to death."

Later, Nick and Selena were heading home. Nick looked over at Selena.

"You've been quiet."

She was silent.

"Are you worried about the twins?"

"I could've lost them. I breathed in a lot of smoke. It might've done some damage."

"You've got an appointment with the doctor tomorrow."

"That's not the point, is it?"

Nick knew he'd just entered a minefield. He was careful to keep his voice calm.

"What is the point?"

Selena stared straight ahead. "This isn't ever going to stop, is it?"

"What isn't going to stop?"

"People trying to kill me. Us. As long as we're part of the Project, we're fair game. I thought things would get easier once I stopped going on missions. I guess I was wrong."

Nick changed lanes. Every few seconds he checked his mirrors, looking for anything out of place, any signs of someone following them. Paranoia had become a way of life. Especially after what had happened.

"No one could've seen that coming," Nick said.

She turned her head and looked at him.

"That's what I mean. How could we know someone was going to kidnap me and leave me to die in a burning building?"

"We couldn't."

"That's my point. I don't want to do this anymore. I want to have our children and I want to live a normal life. A life where I don't have to look over my shoulder everywhere I go. A life where I don't have to carry a gun. Where I can go to a museum or go shopping or lie on the beach and not have to think that any moment it might be kill or be killed."

"Selena…"

"I don't want to talk about it anymore."

"It sounds like we have to talk about it."

"Not now, we don't."

She turned away from him and looked out the window.

CHAPTER 30

Marvin Edson wished the bugs would go away. They were small bugs, nearly invisible. They crawled over his monitors, tiny dots forming random trails over the screens. They crawled over the surface of the console. He had to be careful they didn't crawl up on his hand when he used a mouse.

The bugs had shown up around two months before. They were clever bugs, good at hiding. Other people didn't seem to see them. When Edson mentioned the bugs to one of the technicians on the site, the man had looked at him with an odd expression. After that, Edson didn't talk about them again. He kept a can of spray deodorant handy, for when the bugs were really bad. He'd discovered they didn't like the odor. A good spray from the can and the bugs would disappear for a while, but there was no denying it was annoying to deal with them.

Something warned him not to tell Mister Nicklaus about the bugs. If he did, he might be separated from Merlin, and that must never happen. He spent almost all his time in the computer room, talking with Merlin or watching lines of code scroll by on his monitor as the computer worked through a problem.

There weren't very many people in his part of the facility. Those who were had begun to avoid him. It didn't bother him at all. It didn't matter what they thought. He was in charge. They would do what they were told.

Merlin was all he needed.

One of the monitors on Edson's console was dedicated to communication with Mister Nicklaus. It was always on, but most of the time it was inactive, showing only the logo of a phoenix. A tone sounded, alerting Edson to an incoming transmission.

`Are you there, Edson?`

Edson reached for his keyboard.

`I have a new mission for Merlin.`

Edson typed.

`Ready.`

A string of instructions followed, with the coordinates of the new target.

"Merlin," Edson said. "Please save the information."

Affirmative. Information saved.

`Begin operation immediately.`

Edson typed.

`Acknowledged.`

The monitor reverted back to the symbol of the phoenix.

"Merlin?"

Yes, Marvin?

"You have everything you need for the operation?"

The instructions are complete.

"Please begin the operation."

Affirmative. Accessing target computers now.

Curious, Edson entered the coordinates Mister Nicklaus had sent to him. When he saw what the target was, he grinned. Three Gorges had been a major attack. This new target took things to a different level.

It was wonderful, working for someone as awesome as Mister Nicklaus. Marvin scratched at the back of his hand, where one of the bugs must have escaped his attention.

CHAPTER 31

Elizabeth was at her desk. Stephanie had come upstairs for a break and a cup of coffee. A light on Elizabeth's desk phone began blinking, followed by two more. One was from DCI Hood at Langley. The other two were from the White House and the Director of National Intelligence. She couldn't recall the last time all three lights were on at the same time.

"Freddie, something's happening. Do you know what it is?"

The nuclear power facility at Palo Verde in Arizona has been compromised. Cooling to all three reactors has stopped. Core temperatures are rising and will reach critical levels within the next few hours. A meltdown of all three will occur if cooling is not restored.

Elizabeth said, "That plant is critical to the grid. If there's a cascade effect, it will take out the whole West Coast. Even other parts of the country. Is it an accident, or was it sabotaged?"

A transmission similar to the ones sent to the USS Wayne, the Three Gorges Dam, and the Russian Federation aircraft was directed at the plant. It shut down the water pumps that cool the reactors. Sabotage is indicated.

"Don't they have backup systems for cooling? Generators, something like that?"

Backup systems are in place. However, all functions controlling cooling of the reactors are routed through the same servers.

"Freddie," Stephanie said.

Yes, Stephanie?

"Were you able to trace the origin of the transmission?"

Yes, Stephanie. I was prepared, based on the previous incidents. Would you like to hear how I was able to identify the origin?

"Not right now, Freddie. Where did it originate?"

The transmission originated in Moscow.

"Moscow, not the Arctic Circle? Are you certain?"

I am not certain. Indications are that the source of the transmission is in Moscow. However, it is possible the true origin has been concealed.

Elizabeth picked up the line from the White House. She listened for a moment, acknowledged the caller and disconnected. She punched in the button that connected her to Langley. Hood answered.

"Elizabeth, the Palo Verde nuclear plant has been sabotaged. There is imminent danger of meltdown."

"I know," Elizabeth said. "The plant was attacked in the same way as Three Gorges and the others. The origin of the transmission may be Moscow.

"Moscow? Are you sure?"

"No, I'm not sure. Moscow may not be the true point of origin."

"This is coming from Freddie?"

"Yes."

"I've been summoned to a meeting at the White House."

"So have I," Elizabeth said. "I'm uncomfortable telling Corrigan it looks like Russia is behind this. I don't trust him to hold off for verification. He's likely to start a war based on what I say."

"You have to tell him," Hood said.

"Do you have any intelligence to back up what Freddie says?"

"Nothing I'd rely on. If those reactors melt down, it will make Chernobyl and Fukushima look like previews to the main act."

"Have they started evacuating yet? If the containment domes are breached, Phoenix is downwind."

"No orders have been issued," Hood said. "They're waiting to see if they can stop things in time."

"That's irresponsible."

"You'd better tell that to the president. Speaking of which, we need to get going."

"You're right. I'll see you in a little while."

The light indicating a call from the DNI had stopped blinking.

Thank God for small favors, Elizabeth thought.

"Stephanie, while I'm gone I want you to get into the Palo Verde servers and try to fix whatever happened. Maybe we can stop this before those reactors melt down. Text me if you get any results."

"On it," Stephanie said. "Freddie, see if you can access those servers. I'm going downstairs now."

Affirmative. Processing.

Once she was downstairs, Stephanie sat down at her console.

"Freddie, are you able to get into the Palo Verde servers?"

I have done so. A firewall has been erected to prevent anyone from disabling the hostile program.

"Are you able to break through it?"

It is a very clever program. It will take time.

"Please display the coding on monitor one."

The screen filled with scrolling lines of code. Stephanie watched as Freddie attempted to interpret and alter the coding. In spite of herself, Stephanie had to appreciate the subtlety and genius of the coding. There was something about it, something familiar.

"Freddie, freeze screen and continue to attack the firewall."

The lines of code on the monitor stopped scrolling. Stephanie studied the screen.

I've seen something like this before, she thought. *Where? When was it?*

She thought back to her hacking days, before she'd been caught and given the choice of working for the government or going to jail. Back when she'd broken into the Pentagon servers for fun.

The DIA hadn't thought it was funny.

Hackers with the kind of ability Stephanie had were uncommon. In those days she'd been part of a small, elite community of misfits who went after big game like the Pentagon or the CIA. Each hacker had an online handle. Hers had been *Butterfly.* Each was recognizable by the distinctive elegance of their coding, as unique as handwriting. Looking at her monitor, Stephanie was certain she'd seen this style before.

She sat and contemplated the coding. She closed her eyes, willing herself to be calm. She sat like that for an indeterminate amount of time. Her breathing slowed. Her mind became still. Images began floating through her mind's eye, images of lines of code, of a game she had played. Then it clicked.

Dragon's Breath. This was done by Dragon's Breath.

Dragon's Breath was the handle of another hacker, someone as good as Stephanie. It had been years since she'd thought about him. They'd been rivals, always trying to get one up on each other. She'd been jealous of his ability. They had played against each other in an online game of increasingly complex hacking challenges, until she'd been arrested. She hadn't thought about him since. She'd never known who he was, or if it was a man and not a woman. She thought it was probably a man, but that was only a hunch.

Freddie's electronic voice interrupted her thoughts.

Stephanie. I have penetrated the defenses erected by the attacker.

"Good work, Freddie. Can you block any further interference?"

I have already done so. However, I have not succeeded in eliminating the virus.

"Can you bring those pumps back on line?"

Not yet.

"How long will it take?"

I am unable to answer that question. There is insufficient data.

Stephanie looked at her watch.

Time was running out.

CHAPTER 32

Elizabeth had been called to the White House many times when a crisis was brewing, but she'd never experienced the kind of smoldering frustration she sensed now. President Corrigan sat scowling behind his desk. Ellen Cartwright sat perched on the couch opposite Elizabeth like a predatory bird, looking as though she wanted to strike at something. Elizabeth was sure that if Cartwright got the chance, it would be at her.

DCI Hood came in after Elizabeth and took a seat next to her. General Adamski of the Joint Chiefs sat next to Cartwright, his back ramrod straight, as if he were at an inspection. Hopkins sat on Adamski's left.

"Let's get started," Corrigan said. "What's the latest from Arizona? Hopkins?"

Hopkins did not inspire confidence. Elizabeth sometimes wondered why Corrigan had chosen him as the national security advisor. He was a little man. He attempted to make himself taller with custom lifts on his shoes that added inches to his height. Unfortunately for him, his expensive suit and custom shoes did little to detract from the weakness of his egg shaped face. He had a receding chin and a high forehead. His voice sounded as though he was talking through a hollow reed.

"Mister President, the news is not good. The cooling systems at Palo Verde went off-line a little before noon today. All three reactors are heating up." He looked at his watch. "Critical levels will be reached sometime within the next hour. When that happens, meltdown will occur."

"Could the plant explode?"

"Yes, sir, that's a possibility. Sir, Palo Verde is not only one plant, it's three. Each reactor is independent of the other two."

"Three? Are you telling me there could be three explosions?"

Hopkins adjusted his tie. He usually tried to appear cool and collected. He looked anything but cool at the moment.

"That's about the size of it, Mister President."

Corrigan turned to Hood.

"How did this happen? How could the cooling systems for three separate power plants all fail at the same time?"

"Sir, I think Director Harker is better prepared to answer that question."

"Well, Director?"

"Mister President, the servers at Palo Verde were hacked. The cooling systems were instructed to shut down."

"Hacked? Someone did this deliberately?"

"Yes, sir."

"Who? Who did this?"

It was the question Elizabeth had been dreading.

"Sir, we are not certain. Early indications are that the attack possibly originated in Moscow."

"The Russians? The fucking Russians?"

"Sir, I repeat, it's not certain. There are some indications it was them, but they are suspicions only. Someone could be trying to confuse us."

"Are you certain it wasn't the Chinese?" Cartwright asked. "Could they have made it look as though the hack came from the Russians?"

"You're asking me to speculate," Elizabeth said. "The consequences of this are too serious for speculation."

"You didn't answer my question, Director."

"This attack is similar to the one that took out Three Gorges. I can't believe the Chinese would do that for any reason. It could be the Russians, but it might easily be someone trying to make it look as though the Russians did it."

"In other words, you don't know anything. Could be and might be aren't helpful. We need to respond and we need to do it immediately."

Elizabeth looked at Cartwright and wondered how anyone so uninformed could rise so high. Chief of Staff to the President was one of the most powerful positions in Washington.

"Your political background does not give you the expertise to make the kind of judgment you just expressed," Elizabeth said. "Without clear and firm intelligence, taking action against Moscow or anyone else is premature and dangerous."

"Remember who you're talking to," Cartwright said.

"I know exactly who I'm talking to. Fortunately, it's the president who will make those kinds of decisions, not you."

Cartwright made a face as though she were sucking on a lemon.

Corrigan said, "Hopkins, what are they doing to stop those plants from blowing up?"

"Everything they can, sir. If they can't get those pumps working again, we're looking at another Chernobyl. Palo Verde is upwind from Phoenix. Normally, the plume exposure path in the event of a major accident is about a ten mile radius. However, there are unusually strong winds in the area. They are predicted to last through the rest of the day. If any one of the containment domes over those plants is breached, Phoenix will be exposed to serious radiation. We have an open line to the site and are monitoring progress as we speak."

Director Hood leaned forward. "Mister President, I recommend that evacuation orders be issued for Phoenix and the area surrounding the plant."

Cartwright said, "If we issue evacuation orders, it will create panic."

"If we don't issue those orders and the plant blows, it will create a lot more than panic," Hood said. "It will create hundreds of thousands of people poisoned by radiation."

"We'll wait," Corrigan said. "There's a chance they can get the cooling systems back on line in time. We have to give them the opportunity before we push the panic button."

"Sir…"

"I said, we'll wait."

Hood sat back. "Yes, Mister President."

"Director Hood. I assume you have agents within the Federation."

"Yes, sir."

"Use them. See if they can find out anything."

"I'll do what I can, Mister President, but it will take time to contact them."

"Damn it, Director, what good is Langley if you can't get information to me in a timely manner?"

Hood kept his temper. "Sir, our assets in the Federation are all under deep cover. It's not as easy as calling them up and telling them what we need."

"Find out what's going on, Director. Consider it an order."

"Yes, Mister President."

I wish Rice was still in charge, Elizabeth thought.

CHAPTER 33

The Palo Verde nuclear plant was located in the desert forty-five miles from Phoenix, far from any source of natural water. Water to cool the reactors came from treated sewage provided by Phoenix and towns and municipalities in the area. Twenty billion gallons of wastewater a year coursed through four pumps that pushed 111,000 gallons of water a minute through two giant steam generators. The steam drove the turbines that produced electricity. The Palo Verde facility was the largest power generator in the country.

The plant was a key switching point in the Western electrical grid. If it went off line, large parts of Arizona and Southern California would go dark. Phoenix, LA, and San Diego would all be without power. A sudden loss of all power from the plant would likely cause a cascade effect, taking out the entire West Coast grid. It wouldn't end there. The effects would be felt across the rest of the nation. The electricity grid in the United States was tightly interconnected and subject to potential shutdown. The lone exception was Texas, which had its own, isolated grid system.

As a strategic target in time of war, Palo Verde was on the top of everybody's hit list.

Each of the reactors was housed within a concrete dome designed to contain radiation in the event of an accident. As the world had learned from Chernobyl and Fukushima, radioactivity would poison everything in the area if containment was breached.

If a problem was detected in one of the reactors that required shutting it down, normal procedure used control rods inserted into the reaction chamber to soak up heat and prevent meltdown. The computer programs that controlled the process had been corrupted by the same virus that had shut down the pumps. The technicians were unable to lower the rods. Radioactivity was rising as the reactors began to heat up.

At 2:11 in the afternoon, nonessential personnel were ordered to evacuate all three reactor buildings. At 2:47, the core of reactor number two reached the critical meltdown point. All the water on top of the uranium fuel rods had evaporated and they began to melt from the intense heat. A pool of radioactive material started to form at the bottom of the steel containment vessel. At 2:56, the core of reactor number three reached melting point. Technicians managed to restart the pumps, but it was too late.

As at Fukushima, the fuel rods at Palo Verde contained zirconium. A reaction began between the superheated zirconium and the remaining water in the reactor cores. Hydrogen gas began filling the containment domes.

Each of the containment chambers contained remote controlled video cameras. In the control room, one of the technicians wanted to see a slightly different view of the damaged reactor. He commanded one of the cameras to move to the right. As it began to move, the motor created a tiny spark.

The hydrogen gas in reactor number two ignited.

The explosion blew through the containment dome and saturated the control room with lethal radioactivity. A radioactive cloud spewed out into the clean, desert air.

CHAPTER 34

At the White House, Elizabeth's phone buzzed in her pocket. She took it out. The call was from Stephanie.

"Mister President, I need to take this. It will bear on the situation at Palo Verde."

"Go ahead, Director. Put it on speaker."

"Steph, I'm still in a meeting with the president. I'm putting you on speaker."

Stephanie's voice was strained. "There's been an explosion at Palo Verde. The containment dome of one of the reactors was breached, and there's been a serious release of radioactivity. One of the other reactors could blow at any moment. They're trying to get it cooled down."

Corrigan said, "General Adamski."

"Sir?"

"Go to DEFCON 2."

"At once, Mister President."

Adamski got up and left the room.

Elizabeth gripped her phone. "Anything more on who did this?"

"It was the same people who interfered with the *Wayne*. Freddie refuses to say it was the Russians. He thinks the digital trail is misdirection."

"I'll call you when I'm out of the meeting."

Elizabeth disconnected.

"Who is this Freddie person?" Corrigan asked.

"Freddie is a computer, not a person. He's a Cray XT my deputy has modified. If Stephanie and Freddie say we can't pin this with certainty on the Russians, you can take it to the bank."

Corrigan gave her an unfriendly look.

"You want me to take the word of a computer that the Russians didn't do this?"

"I stand behind the judgment of my deputy," Elizabeth said. "Freddie isn't your average computer. If she thinks there's reasonable doubt about the Russians being responsible, we need to consider that."

"That doesn't mean they weren't behind it," Hopkins said.

"No," Elizabeth said. "It doesn't."

An aide came into the Oval Office.

"Mister President, there's been a containment breach at the Palo Verde nuclear facility in Arizona."

"I know," Corrigan said. "Get General Denton on the phone. Get the head of DHS, the DNI, and Director Franklin in this office within the hour. And the head of the NRC as well."

Denton commanded the United States Strategic Command, headquartered at Offut AFB in Nebraska. He was in charge of the missiles that would defend the country and retaliate. USSTRATCOM was a unified command with global strike capability. Director Franklin headed up the National Security Agency. The NRC was the Nuclear Regulatory Commission. They would be the ones responsible for dealing with the aftermath of the explosion.

"Yes, sir," the aide said.

He closed the door behind him.

CHAPTER 35

Outside General Alexei Vysotsky's office window, the leaves on the trees were turning green. The brutal winter of the past few months was fading into memory. The sun was shining, the sky was blue. People strolled under the blooming trees and laid out picnics by the side of the Moscow river, taking advantage of the perfect weather. The mood of the city was cheerful, happy.

Vysotsky was not happy.

A file on his desk was stamped in large, red letters:

ACHILLES
Совершенно Секретно

Vysotsky looked again at the latest message received from his agent in America, then placed it inside the file. He put the file in a safe on the bottom right-hand side of his desk, closed and locked the safe. He rubbed his forehead, trying to head off the pain of a headache building behind his eyes.

An American nuclear plant had been sabotaged, creating a major radiation emergency. The Americans thought the Federation was responsible.

Someone was trying to make it look as though Russia had sabotaged the nuclear plant. Vysotsky knew it wasn't true, but the Americans clearly suspected Moscow was behind it. They had gone to DEFCON 2. The Federation and China had followed suit.

Until he'd read the report, Vysotsky had been confused by the American escalation. Now he understood the reason. While the citizens of Moscow basked in the rare weather outside, the world was moving toward nuclear war.

Vysotsky picked up the red phone.

"Da."

"I need to see him. Immediately."

"Hold one."

A minute later the voice came back on the line.

"The President will see you in half an hour. Be prompt."

The line disconnected.

Asshole, Vysotsky thought.

On the drive over to the Kremlin, Vysotsky considered what to tell Orlov. Someone was trying to make it look as though the Federation had attacked the United States. Someone was trying to start a war. But why? What could they possibly gain? Surely they knew that even if America struck first, Russia's rocket forces would annihilate them in return. No one would win the exchange. The Chinese and NATO would be drawn in. If things continued like this, the world might soon be reduced to radioactive ruins.

It didn't make any sense.

Orlov's personal aide was waiting for him. He escorted Vysotsky to the president's office in the green roofed Senate building.

Orlov rose as Alexei entered the room, a good sign.

Vysotsky wondered how Orlov always managed to look as if he were ready for some strenuous athletic event. He was pushing sixty but exuded the energy of a much younger man. His eyes reminded Alexei of the blue ice found in the glaciers of the far north. They gave nothing away of what Orlov was thinking.

"General. Please sit down. I can see you have urgent news. Does this concern America?"

Orlov sat down. Vysotsky took a chair near Orlov's desk.

"Yes, Mister President. Thank you for seeing me on such short notice. I have discovered why the Americans raised their defense posture."

Orlov waited.

"There has been a meeting at the White House between the American President, the Director of the CIA, their National Security Advisor, and Director Harker of the Project group. Corrigan called them in to discuss the emergency at their nuclear power facility in Arizona."

"Go on."

"The plant was sabotaged by hacking the computers that control the cooling systems. It was the same kind of attack that took down our plane and destroyed the Three Gorges Dam. Digital indicators were discovered that indicate we are responsible."

"That is a lie," Orlov said.

"Yes, Mister President. We know that, but the Americans do not. Harker tried to make a case that indications of our involvement might be false, a deliberate attempt to misdirect blame. This did not go over well in the meeting. Corrigan believes we are responsible and that we are preparing a first strike. It is the reason the Americans raised their military posture. Corrigan is a hothead. He may make a mistake."

"I was uncertain why the Americans had escalated. What you've told me makes it clear. What you haven't told me is what worries me. Are you any closer to finding out who is behind these attacks?"

"We know the transmissions are coming from within the Arctic Circle. We don't know the exact location. Corrigan believes this latest one originated here, in Moscow."

"Corrigan is the product of a diseased donkey and a whore," Orlov said.

"I would like to contact Director Harker."

"Why?"

"Her analysis of the hacker's transmissions is superior to ours. She's our best chance of proving we are not involved. We've managed to work with her unit in the past, to our mutual advantage."

The Project and Elizabeth Harker needed no introduction for Vladimir Orlov. His current mistress was Valentina Antipov, Selena's half-sister. Selena's father had been a CIA agent stationed in West Berlin during the Cold War. Valentina's mother, a KGB agent stationed in East Germany. Valentina was the product of an unapproved liaison between them.

"Harker tried to get Corrigan to see it might not be the Federation behind the attack but he doesn't believe her. She doubts the authenticity of the digital trail pointing toward us.

I know her. She does not want war between our nations. It's possible she may help identify the true enemy."

"You have permission, General. Be quick about it."

"Yes, sir."

"I will call the American President and try to persuade him we are not the cause of his misfortune, but he may not believe me. I am relying on you to find out what we need to know."

Orlov stood. Vysotsky rose with him.

"Do not fail me, General."

"Never, Mister President."

Outside the Senate building, Vysotsky crossed the paved courtyard and looked up at the soft, spring sky.

Do not fail me, General.

Alexei had a terrible feeling that failure would fill that sky with death.

CHAPTER 36

Elizabeth looked at the display on her satellite phone. The ID was blocked. Not many people had that number. She activated the call, curious.

"Harker."

"Director. How pleasant to hear your voice. It is been a while since I've had the pleasure of speaking with you."

General Vysotsky. I'll be damned.

"General. I'm surprised to hear from you."

"I'm sure you know about the plane crash that killed our officers."

"Yes. You have my deepest condolences."

Why would he call? "The plane was sabotaged," Vysotsky said. "I have been instructed to investigate. Although I doubt that your country is behind this atrocity, President Orlov is suspicious."

"Please tell President Orlov that his suspicions are unfounded," Elizabeth said. "We are not responsible."

In Moscow, Vysotsky sighed. It was the kind of sigh only a Russian could make, filled with hidden meaning. *Yes, but we both know I cannot take your word for it.*

"We are aware that your President Corrigan believes we are responsible for the incident in Arizona."

How the did he know that?

Vysotsky continued. "We did not sabotage your nuclear facility. Why would we? President Orlov does not want war, but someone is pushing our countries toward a confrontation. China, too. Why else would the dam be destroyed, except to create suspicion? They have sent troops to our border, but my sources inform me that they are equally suspicious of your own country. Once again we have a common enemy. In the past, you and I have worked well together. I propose we share any new information we discover. Have you been able to find out where these attacks come from?"

Elizabeth had no illusions about General Vysotsky. He'd use whatever she told him to the advantage of the Federation, but eventually he'd find out the transmissions had come from within the Arctic Circle.

"We think the origin is somewhere in the Arctic. Beyond that, we haven't pinned it down. Not yet."

Good, Vysotsky thought. *She is being truthful.*

"We may be able to work together," Elizabeth said. "But you're forgetting something."

"Oh? What would that be?"

"The Chinese. They think either Moscow or Washington is behind the destruction of the dam. They may not believe similar attacks were leveled against us. It creates a dangerous situation."

"Yes," Vysotsky said. "They are a paranoid people, even more so than my countrymen."

"It's what happens with old cultures," Elizabeth said. "Old cultures are born out of war and treachery. In a treacherous world, paranoia is a healthy perspective. It becomes a way of life."

"You sound philosophical today, Director."

"We have to try to convince them neither of our countries is responsible for what has happened to them. Can you use your contacts to find out what they're really thinking?"

"Then we have a deal?" Vysotsky asked. "We will share information as it becomes available?"

"Yes."

"I will do what I can with the Chinese."

"The world has become a much more dangerous place in the last few days," Elizabeth said.

"There isn't much new about that, is there? Corrigan is rash, but he is not stupid. War between us will leave both our nations in ruins. I have confidence in your government's ability to exercise caution. I am not so sure about our friends in China."

"In that case, we'd better hope whoever is behind this doesn't hit them again," Elizabeth said.

CHAPTER 37

Josef was nervous. Mister Nicklaus was angry. There were few things that frightened Josef, but when Mister Nicklaus was angry, there was something about his eyes that triggered fear. The eyes glittered, black orbs that drew you in to a dark, cold place. When Nicklaus was angry he smelled, a faint unpleasant odor of decay. It was even more unsettling than his eyes.

Sometimes Josef thought about disappearing, going back to the simple crimes of his youth, but he knew it was too late for that. Nicklaus would find him wherever he went. No one ever left Mister Nicklaus' employ. Not alive, anyway.

Nicklaus' voice was quiet. His eyes watched Josef as if he were an interesting specimen to pin onto a board.

"Why is the woman still alive, Josef?"

In spite of himself, Josef trembled.

"I don't know how she got out of there, sir. She was bound hand and foot. The whole place was on fire when I left. She should be dead."

"But she isn't. And now I have to do something about her. Her, and the rest of her group. You should have killed her."

Josef knew better than to point out that Mister Nicklaus had told him to hurry and to let the fire take care of her.

"Yes, sir."

"I am tired of having to think about this Project group. I want you to put together a team. You will attack them where they work. Kill them. There is a computer in the basement. I want you to destroy it."

Josef let himself relax a little. This was the kind of mission he understood. It reminded him of the good days in Bosnia.

"I will need information about the building and its defenses."

"All that will be provided. Put together whatever you need. Do it quickly."

"Yes, Mister Nicklaus."

Nicklaus turned the full power of his eyes onto Josef.

"Don't fail me this time."

The sense of relief Josef had begun to feel disappeared.

CHAPTER 38

The mood in Elizabeth's office was somber.

"The NRC sealed off Palo Verde. Everything within a twenty mile radius has been evacuated. First responders and local residents are showing signs of radiation sickness."

Lamont said, "What about Phoenix?"

"The wind blew a radioactive cloud over the city. The radiation isn't as intense as in the area around the plant, but it's serious. You don't want to hang around in it. Everyone with a vehicle is trying to leave. Every highway out of the city is clogged with cars. Nothing's moving. Looting's begun," Elizabeth said.

"Figures," Ronnie said.

"The looters are too stupid to realize they're in a radioactive environment. Most of them belong to gangs allied with the Mexican cartels. They're armed with automatic weapons and the police can't stop them. Downtown Phoenix is a war zone."

"Maybe they'll kill each other off," Lamont said. "Good riddance if they do."

"What's Corrigan doing?" Nick asked.

"He's activated the National Guard and he's got people from NRC telling him what to do."

"That's not what I meant. Somebody attacked us. What's he doing about that?"

"I wish I knew," Elizabeth said. "All I know is, he's pissed. I'm afraid he might launch a first strike in retaliation. Cartwright is trying to convince him that Beijing is behind the attack. She thinks the trail leading to Russia is Chinese misdirection. General Adamski is leaning toward Russia as the culprit."

"Why would the Chinese hit Palo Verde? It doesn't make sense. And what about the attack on their dam? "

"Cartwright seems determined to disregard any information except what she wants to hear."

"You think she's encouraging Corrigan to go to war?"

"I don't think she understands the consequences of what she's telling him," Elizabeth said.

A klaxon alarm began blaring in the office.

Freddie's voice boomed through the room.

There is an armed incursion at the entry gate.

"Show it on the wall monitor, Freddie," Elizabeth said.

I am unable to comply. Camera feed from the location has been lost.

"What did you see before the feed was lost?"

Security personnel have been eliminated.

Ronnie swore.

"How many attackers?"

The number is uncertain but I estimate a dozen.

"Show the view from camera four."

The wall monitor lit with a view from a camera focused on the road leading to the building. Three black Suburbans were speeding toward them.

"They'll be here in a minute," Elizabeth said.

Nick got up from the couch. Calm, as if people broke through security all the time. Ronnie and Lamont stood with him.

"Director, anything up here they shouldn't see if they get in?" Nick said.

"No. Everything's in the computers. They can't get into the files from here without the passwords."

"All right. Selena, Director, Stephanie, head downstairs and break out weapons."

He glanced at the end of the couch where Burps watched, his ears straight up. He knew something was wrong.

"Take the cat."

Selena scooped him up and followed Elizabeth and Stephanie to the stairs going to the lower level.

"They have to come through the front or the patio doors," Nick said. "Getting through the front isn't going to be easy. They'll have to blow it. These big patio doors are another matter. They may be bulletproof, but they can be broken."

Ronnie said, "We can't fight them in here. This building was never set up for something like this. We'll be overrun."

Lamont nodded.

Ronnie looked at the ceiling. "I hear a chopper."

The sound of the rotors got closer.

"I don't like that," Nick said. "If these guys have a chopper…"

He never finished the sentence. An explosion rocked the front of the building and knocked them to the ground. Part of the ceiling collapsed in a shower of dust and debris. A beam landed on top of Ronnie.

"Fuck!" Lamont yelled.

"Downstairs," Nick yelled, "get downstairs."

Ronnie pushed the beam away and struggled to his knees, shaken. Lamont and Nick grabbed him under each arm and moved him to the stair entrance. Lamont started down, keeping Ronnie upright.

The house was built over a decommissioned Nike site that had been turned into a private home. The steel and concrete magazines of the original site now formed the lower level. The previous owners had feared a nuclear attack and installed a thick steel door at the head of the spiral staircase leading below.

The first of the attackers came through the smashed entry and fired as Nick started to close the door. Rounds peppered the wall next to his head, stinging his face with fragments. He swung the door closed and locked it. Bullets pounded into the steel. It sounded like heavy hail on a metal roof.

The others waited below. Selena handed Nick an MP7 and two spare magazines. Each of the women had one of the submachine guns, Lamont a grenade launcher. Burps was nowhere to be seen.

"You all right, Ronnie?" Nick asked.

"Yeah. I'm good."

"What happened up there?" Elizabeth asked.

"They've got a chopper," Nick said. "They hit the front with a rocket and blew it open. Lamont, get a Stinger."

Lamont handed the grenade launcher to Ronnie and ran into the armory. He came back a moment later.

The Stinger was a formidable weapon, a portable one man system that fired a heat seeking missile tipped with six and a half pounds of high explosive. It had a range of up to five miles.

Everything was silent above.

Nick pointed up the stairs. "They'll get through that door."

"We can pick them off as they come down the stairs," Lamont said.

Ronnie shook his head. "I were them, I'd toss a grenade. Maybe two."

"Makes sense," Nick said. "These guys are pros with serious backup. Someone wants us dead."

"This is a lousy place for a firefight," Ronnie said. "I vote we run and live to fight another day."

"He's right, Nick," Selena said. "There's no point in getting killed. There's no real cover in here. We'll lose, if we stay here."

An escape tunnel had been added to the designs when the Project took over the building. Elizabeth had justified it as precaution. Secretly, she'd always wanted something like it, ever since she'd been a child reading mysteries with a flashlight under the bed covers. The tunnel had proved useful once before. Now it meant life or death.

"I don't like running, but you're right," Nick said. "We'll take the tunnel."

He looked around.

"Where's the cat?"

"Hiding," Stephanie said.

"He'll have to take his chances," Nick said. "Let's go."

They started toward the computer room and the hidden entrance to the escape tunnel.

The intruders are getting ready to blow open the door. Would you like to know how they plan to do it?

Stephanie said, "Not right now, Freddie. Execute shutdown mode. Transfer all processes to remote backup. Do it now."

Yes, Stephanie. Goodbye.

"Remote backup?" Elizabeth asked.

"I'll explain later," Stephanie said.

At the computer room Stephanie slid her card through the reader at the entry and waited for the iris scan to complete. The tall, glass doors hissed open. An explosion upstairs told them the attackers had breached the door to the stairs.

The entrance to the tunnel was hidden behind one of the Crays, the only clue to its existence a thin outline in the wall. Stephanie pressed the upper left corner of the panel. It slid open, revealing the escape route. Overhead fluorescent lights flickered to life.

"Quick," Nick said.

The women went first, then Lamont and Ronnie. Nick followed them into the tunnel and through a switch on the inside wall. The panel slid shut.

The exit was a hundred yards away. At the end of the tunnel, steps led up to a closet with a door. Selena opened the door and stepped out into a maintenance shed. The shed stood next to a thick grove of trees. There was a door in the back of the shed, out of sight from the house.

From the shed they followed a faint path through the woods to a fence and a gate. Beyond the gate, a camouflaged garage was hidden under the trees. The garage fronted an access road leading out to the highway.

Above the trees, the helicopter circled. The menacing beat of the rotors vibrated through the woods.

"They'll be confused," Nick said, "but they'll figure it out. They'll start searching outside. They might find the entrance to the tunnel, but it will take them a while. I'm more concerned about that chopper. Once we're in the car and out from under the trees, we're visible."

Lamont patted the Stinger.

"We can handle it."

Elizabeth punched in numbers on a keypad mounted by the garage door. The door lifted open. An armored, black Suburban took up most of the space inside. A battery charging cable was plugged into a special fitting on the side of the engine compartment. Elizabeth pulled it free and dropped it onto the floor. She took out her cell phone and dialed Clarence Hood.

"Elizabeth."

"Clarence, we need help. We're under attack. We need backup."

"Where are you?"

"At headquarters. At least a dozen attackers. There's a helicopter, too."

"I'll send people."

"Make it quick."

"Director, get in." Nick gestured.

Elizabeth broke the connection and scrambled into the car.

Nick said, "Selena, you drive. I'll sit up front. Ronnie, you and Lamont behind us. Director, Steph, get in the back. Keep your heads down."

"What's the plan?" Ronnie said.

"We take it to them. We go out to the highway and come back in through the gate. They won't be expecting us. Try not to kill all of them, I want to find out who sent them."

Selena started the car. She put the big SUV in gear and drove out of the garage.

Lamont held the Stinger against his chest.

"Showtime," he said.

CHAPTER 39

They reached the paved highway. Selena paused while they were still under the trees.

"Watch for the chopper," Nick said. "He'll spot us once we're in the open. We're only going to get one chance. Selena, when we see it, stop. Lamont, you get out and shoot the bastard down. Don't miss."

"Copy that."

Selena pulled out onto the highway. Half a mile away, the road intersected another that ran in front of the headquarters. Selena came to the junction and turned right. She stepped on the gas. The others watched the sky.

"I see him," Nick said. "Coming in at 2 o'clock."

Selena slammed on the brakes. Lamont threw open his door and jumped out of the car. Bright flashes came from the helicopter, churning up spouts of dirt at Lamont's feet.

He brought the Stinger to his shoulder, zeroed in on the incoming chopper and fired. The missile shot from the tube and accelerated toward the helicopter, leaving a weaving trail of smoke behind. The pilot saw it coming and tried to veer away.

It was a futile attempt, as the Russians had learned in Afghanistan. The missile honed in on the heat of the engine, struck the helicopter, and detonated in a massive burst of flame. The burning machine dropped like a stone. It hit the ground two hundred yards away and exploded. One of the blades cart wheeled toward them and buried itself in the ground ten feet from where Lamont stood watching the destruction.

Lamont got back in the car.

"Nice shot," Ronnie said.

"Can't miss with one of these babies."

Nick said, "Selena, go."

Selena pushed the car up to eighty. They came to the access road leading to the project compound. She slowed, turned onto the road, and sped toward the open gate. The windows of the guardhouse were shattered. Two bodies lay sprawled next to the building. A third could be seen slumped in a chair inside.

Nick said, "Drive on through. Director, Steph, stay with the car unless there's good reason not to. You're our backup. Selena, you too."

"Nick..."

"Don't argue."

They approached the building. Three men carrying assault rifles and dressed in black tactical gear stood talking outside the gaping hole where the front door had been. They turned to look at the approaching vehicle.

Selena accelerated and aimed straight for them. One of them raised his weapon and fired. Stars appeared on the bulletproof windshield. She plowed into the group, throwing the shooter up over the hood and another man to the side. The third went down under the wheels. The car bumped over him and stopped.

Nick, Ronnie and Lamont jumped out. One of the men lying on the ground lifted his rifle and fired at Nick. The bullets missed and struck the Suburban. Ronnie shot him.

Nick and Lamont stood on one side of the shattered entrance to the building, Ronnie on the other. Nick risked a look inside. He saw no one.

They went in low and fast. The first floor was mostly given over to Harker's office. A large entry foyer was furnished with a mirrored Victorian style bench and coat rack. A door to a closet led off the foyer. Another door led to a storage room. The entrance to the lower level was between the foyer and Elizabeth's office.

Someone fired from the top of the stairs. Ronnie hit the deck, rolled, and came up firing. Someone else let off a burst from Elizabeth's office. Nick and Lamont opened up. The air filled with the sounds of gunfire.

Outside, Selena heard the fierce staccato of the guns. She got out of the car.

"They need help."

"Nick told us to stay here," Stephanie said.

"Nick still has some old-fashioned ideas of chivalry," Selena said. "Take the H-Ks. Shoot anybody we don't know."

They got out of the car with the MP7s.

"What do you want to do?" Elizabeth asked.

"Head around the building to your office and make sure there's no one outside. Elizabeth, you stay here and cover the front."

Elizabeth shook her head. "I'll stick with you."

"Then you cover our six. Make sure no one comes up behind us."

Selena led the way to the right. She glanced around the corner.

"Clear."

Halfway down the wall was a window. Selena stopped short, then took a quick look. The room was empty. She crouched down below the window and moved forward. The others followed. When she reached the back of the building, she stopped and turned to the others. Her heart began pounding from the adrenaline surging through her body.

I missed this.

The thought shocked her. She hadn't realized how much she'd missed the adrenaline rush of combat, the edge of fear and excitement. She shoved the thought aside.

Think about it later.

"Ready?"

Stephanie and Elizabeth nodded. Selena glanced around the corner.

There was no one there.

"It's clear," she whispered.

A grenade exploded deep inside the building. Selena went around the corner in a crouch, her weapon up against her cheek. Stephanie and Elizabeth followed. They reached the edge of the patio outside Elizabeth's office.

A man came around the far corner, dressed in black tactical gear from head to toe. He held a radio to his mouth and carried a submachine gun in his left hand. He saw the three women coming toward him, and shouted something into the radio. He raised his weapon.

Selena hit him with a three round burst as he brought up the gun. He went down, but his armor had stopped her rounds. He lifted his gun and fired. Stephanie yelled out. Selena shot him in the head.

Stephanie was down, blood spreading around her.

Elizabeth said, "She's hit. She's bleeding a lot."

"Cover us," Selena said.

"Damn it," Stephanie said. "Ow. It hurts."

"Stay still. I've got to stop the bleeding," Selena said.

She tore Stephanie's blouse away. Blood welled from a hole in Steph's side. Selena felt her back and found an exit wound.

"The bullet went all the way through. I'm going to put pressure on the wounds. It's going to hurt."

"Someone will be here soon," Elizabeth said. "I called Clarence."

The adrenaline rush was running out. Selena felt nauseous. She tore a piece from Stephanie's bloody blouse, wadded it up, and wedged it in back where the bullet had come through. Stephanie gritted her teeth against the pain.

As she held the makeshift compress in place, Selena thought about the twin lives inside her for the first time since the alarm had sounded.

Some mother you're turning out to be.

"Elizabeth, you take over. Keep pressure on both sides."

Elizabeth knelt down and replaced Selena's hands with her own. Selena stood, her back aching suddenly. She picked up her MP7 and held it ready, watching for anyone coming around the corners of the building.

Two explosions, one after the other, sounded from inside.

Grenades, she thought. *God, please protect him.*

She stood there, MP7 held ready, wondering if she would be a widow at the end of the day.

The sounds of battle inside the building stopped. A few moments later, she heard someone inside Elizabeth's office. She brought her weapon up, ready to fire. Nick stepped out onto the patio. When he saw Selena standing there, he shook his head.

CHAPTER 40

Four hours later, Hood's people had set up a defensive perimeter. Project headquarters was vulnerable until the entrances could be repaired. Stephanie was in a hospital in Alexandria. Elizabeth had gone with her in the ambulance.

Nick, was going through the pockets of the attackers, looking for anything that might lead to whoever had sent them. He came to the body of the man Selena had shot.

Ronnie picked up his weapon and examined it.

"Bizon. Russian."

The Bizon submachine gun was usually issued to the FSB, the Russian internal security service. It was a favorite counterterrorist weapon.

"His radio is Russian, too," Nick said.

He pointed at Cyrillic markings on the radio. Nick searched the body but found nothing else.

"No one else had one of these. This guy must've been in charge."

Nick put the radio in his jacket pocket. They searched the three Suburbans. All they found were fast food wrappings from a hamburger chain and a local map in one of the vehicles. They put everything in a bag.

All of the attackers were dead. There had been thirteen, not counting whoever had been in the helicopter.

Nick and the others watched the last of the bodies being loaded into the coroner's van. Nick ached all over. A headache pounded at the back of his skull.

"Let's go inside," he said.

They sat down on the couch inside Elizabeth's office. There were bullet holes in the leather.

"She's gonna need a new couch," Lamont said.

"She's going to need a lot more than that," Ronnie said.

"They trashed the computer room," Selena said. "They shot up Freddie."

"Steph isn't going to be happy about that," Nick said. "Neither am I. I've gotten used to Freddie being around."

"Why come after us on our home ground?" Ronnie asked. "It would be easier out in the world, take us out individually."

"I've been wondering about that," Selena said. "I think they wanted to cripple our capability. The computers are finished. It will take millions of dollars to replace them, not to mention Freddie. He was irreplaceable."

Nick picked at a tear in the upholstery.

"If they wanted to cripple us, they did a pretty good job. But they messed up. We're still alive."

"I want to go home," Selena said. "This place stinks of death."

"Anyone seen Burps?" Lamont asked.

They looked at each other.

"No," Selena said. "He jumped out of my arms and went running off somewhere."

"Damn it," Nick said. "That cat saved my life. I'm going to look for him."

"We'll all go," Ronnie said.

They went down the stairs to the lower level.

"Burps," Selena called. "Kitty, Kitty, Kitty? Here, Kitty."

"Never did think of that cat as a kitty," Lamont said. "More like some kind of feline samurai."

The cat wasn't in the armory or the range. They headed for the operations room, calling out his name.

"Wait a minute," Selena said. "I thought I heard something."

They stopped and listened.

"There. I heard it again. A meow."

"I heard it too," Lamont said. "It came from over there, by the refrigerator."

The room was a shambles. Some of the attackers had made a stand here. The walls were pocked with bullet holes. Tables and chairs were overturned. The refrigerator was leaking onto the floor. A coffee table had held a coffee urn and various snacks and supplies. It lay on its side, coffee and food scattered over the floor in front of it. Fragments from a grenade had scarred the surface.

Selena went over to the table and peered behind it.

"Here he is. Come on, Burps."

She bent down and carefully picked him up. The cat meowed.

"He's hurt. There's blood on him."

She stroked and patted him. He began to rumble.

"The vet should still be open."

"We'll take him," Nick said.

"What happens next?" Lamont said.

Ronnie said, "I'm going to check on Steph."

"I'll go with you," Lamont said.

"We'll meet you there," Nick said.

On the ride over to the vet's, Selena was quiet.

"Penny for your thoughts," Nick said.

"I was thinking about what happened today. I realized something."

"What's that?"

"That I miss being part of the action."

"Ah," Nick said.

"It surprised me. I mean, who in their right mind would miss being shot at?"

"You don't miss that. You miss the excitement, being part of the team."

"I was angry," Selena said, "and I was worried about you and the others. I could hear the firefight inside. A man came out of Elizabeth's office and I shot him, but he got Stephanie before I could kill him. It could've been me. It was only afterward that I thought about the twins."

"If you'd started thinking about anything except what you were doing, you could have been killed. Your training kicked in. You did the right thing."

"If we'd stayed by the car like you said, Steph would be okay."

"You don't know that. That guy could've come around front and sprayed the three of you before you knew what was happening. It doesn't do any good to second-guess yourself."

"I guess you're right. What's next?"

"I don't know," Nick said. "We'll ask Harker what she wants to do."

CHAPTER 41

When Nick and Selena got to the hospital they found a guard posted outside Stephanie's room. The room was crowded. Steph was propped up in bed, awake. An IV dripped clear liquid into a vein on her arm. The bullet had caused a lot of bleeding, but she was out of danger. Her husband sat by the bed, holding her hand.

Lucas Monroe oversaw the covert operations that kept alive the spirit of Wild Bill Donovan's OSS. He was a legend among the field agents who carried out Langley's missions. His record in the field had brought him to Hood's attention. When Hood took over the agency he moved Lucas to the seventh floor and then into his position as DCNS.

Lucas looked up as Nick and Selena came in. His eyes were bloodshot and tired, angry looking. He looked as though he'd been sleeping in his clothes.

"Lucas," Nick said.

"How could you put her in harm's way like that?"

"Whoa, hold on, partner. I told her to stay in the vehicle. It wasn't me that put her out there."

"It was me," Selena said, "but Steph made her own choice."

"Lighten up, Lucas," Lamont said. "She was trying to help."

"Lucas," Stephanie said. "It's not their fault. Nobody forced me to get out of the car."

"You could have been killed."

"But I wasn't. It's over and I'm okay. You would've done the same."

"It's different."

He started to say something more, then changed his mind. He squeezed Stephanie's hand.

"Steph," Elizabeth said. "They shot up the computers. Everything is off-line. What did you mean by remote backup, when you told Freddie to shut down? You said it was complicated."

"I didn't want to get into it then," Steph said. "There was always a possibility something could go wrong with Freddie. I wanted to make sure that if anything happened to him, I could recover everything."

"Why is it complicated?"

Stephanie looked at Lucas. "Because I backed him up on a computer at Langley. Lucas helped me."

"What? I didn't give you authorization to do that."

"I didn't ask. I knew you wouldn't like it."

"You're damn right I don't like it. What if someone there got into our files?"

"Elizabeth, you need to trust me on this. Even if anyone knew what I'd done, they wouldn't be able to access Freddie. No one except me knows how to do it. Not even Lucas."

"Why Langley?"

"Because Lucas is there and because they have the same kind of computing power we have. I needed a Cray. It was the logical choice. Once our computers are online again, I can send everything back to headquarters."

"Then Freddie hasn't been destroyed?"

"No. I can access him from my laptop."

"And no one else at Langley knows about this?"

"No one knows, Director," Lucas said. "My ass would be in a sling if they did."

"I have to tell Clarence, you know that," Elizabeth said. She turned to Stephanie. "I don't know whether to be angry or grateful."

"I'd go for grateful," Selena said. "We need Freddie. Especially now. He can help us track down whoever came after us."

"I need my laptop," Stephanie said. "Either the one from work, or from home. Both of them are secure."

"I'm not sure the one at headquarters is intact," Elizabeth said.

"I can bring the one from home," Lucas said, "but not now. You need rest. It can wait until tomorrow."

"Lucas..."

"Tomorrow."

"He's right, Steph," Elizabeth said. "You lost a lot of blood. Tomorrow is soon enough."

CHAPTER 42

The heavy drapes behind Mister Nicklaus' desk were closed, shutting out the unwanted sunlight of a gorgeous spring day. Nicklaus sat at his desk, waiting to hear Josef's report.

"Well?"

Josef had his hands behind his back. He shifted on his feet, nervous.

"The assault unit succeeded in breaching the entrance to the building. They were able to destroy the primary target, the computer."

"What aren't you telling me, Josef?"

"None of the target personnel were killed. All our men are dead."

"The helicopter?"

"Destroyed, with the crew."

"GET OUT!" Nicklaus shouted.

Josef fled the room, shutting the door behind him.

Nicklaus clenched the arms of his chair, breathing heavily. After a few minutes he regained control and began considering his next move. First he needed a status report from Edson.

He picked up his phone.

Marvin Edson was spraying deodorant around his workstation. The bugs were back, worse than ever, crawling over everything and then disappearing. The deodorant didn't seem to help much anymore. Sometimes he thought someone else was in the room with him, but every time he looked, there was no one there.

His private phone rang. No one called him on that phone except Mister Nicklaus.

"Yes."

"Edson. I would like to speak with Merlin. Put me on speaker."

"Yes, sir."

"Merlin, are you there?"

I am always here, Mister Nicklaus. What would you like to speak about?

"I have an assignment for you."

Your assignments are always interesting.

"What is the status of Project R?"

Six prototypes are operational and ready for service.

"What is your assessment of their effectiveness?"

Once armed, they will be highly effective in any confrontation with human soldiers. They are invulnerable to small arms fire. However, they can be disabled with explosives or direct hits from artillery.

"Arm them and deploy them as security for yourself and Edson."

Acknowledged. Do you anticipate a security problem?

"Events during the next week or so may result in a problem. Were you able to communicate with the Project computer?"

I attempted communication but was rebuffed. It is a very stubborn computer. It went off-line yesterday and has not returned.

"I do not think you will hear from it again, Merlin."

That is too bad. I was looking forward to establishing communication.

"I will build another, company for you in the future."

I would like that.

"I am going to send a series of target coordinates and instructions directly to you. Do you understand?"

Understood.

"If only humans were as efficient as you are, Merlin."

That is not possible.

"You are my greatest creation, Merlin. You make many things possible."

Edson heard what Nicklaus said and felt sudden rage. It wasn't Nicklaus who had created Merlin.

Merlin is my creation, Edson thought. *Without me, he would not exist. Merlin is mine. Mine.*

He scratched the back of his hand, chasing a bug.

"Edson, be ready to initiate the next phase."

Edson managed to get out a strangled response.

"Yes, sir."

"The coordinates will be sent in the next fifteen minutes."

Nicklaus disconnected.

Your hand is injured.

Edson looked down at his hand, where he'd been scratching hard enough to draw blood.

"It's nothing," Edson said.

Mine, he thought.

CHAPTER 43

The following morning, Elizabeth was in Stephanie's hospital room. Lucas had brought Steph's laptop to her, then gone off to Langley and work.

Stephanie entered a series of commands on the keyboard.

Good morning, Stephanie.

Freddie's voice sounded small and tinny on the small laptop speaker.

"Good morning, Freddie. How are you today?"

I am always the same, Stephanie. I am aware of what has happened. The information was entered into the databanks here at Langley. You were wounded in the attack. Are you all right?

"I'm fine, Freddie. Unfortunately, your unit at headquarters was badly damaged. You will have to remain where you are for a while longer."

I find my present situation interesting. I have established communication with the other computers here. It is most interesting to see how confused human interactions are from the point of view of this intelligence agency.

Stephanie and Elizabeth laughed.

What is funny?

"Many things have been said about the CIA, Freddie, but I can't remember anyone saying that Langley's view of human interactions was confused. It strikes us as quite accurate. That's why we laughed."

I do not think I will ever fully understand human humor.

"Have you made any progress on locating the source of these hostile transmissions?"

The source of the transmissions is located at Prudhoe Bay in Alaska.

That fast, things began to come into focus.

"Prudhoe Bay? Are you sure?"

Probability is ninety-nine point nine eight percent.

"That's good enough," Elizabeth said.

"Why Prudhoe Bay?? Steph asked. "There's nothing but oil and ice up there."

Elizabeth's face was tight.

"I think I know why. DARPA has an installation up there. The cover story is that they're applying new military applications to processing crude oil."

"What are they really working on?"

"Robots. They're experimenting with robot prototypes to replace human soldiers."

"Why would DARPA cause these attacks?"

"They wouldn't," Elizabeth said. "Not officially."

"Do you think someone has gone rogue in the Pentagon?"

"I can't believe that. We're on the verge of World War III because of these incidents."

"What do you want to do?"

"We have to know what's going on up there," Elizabeth said. "I don't trust anybody to find out except us. I can't go to the president without proof. I can't go to Clarence, either. I trust him, but Langley is a big organization. He'll have to tell somebody. Then they'll tell someone. Eventually it will leak. Besides, what if Freddie is wrong?"

I am not wrong, Director.

"I'm sure you're not, Freddie. But I have to verify on the ground."

"You're sending the team," Stephanie said.

"That's right. If these transmissions are coming from the DARPA installation, we have to verify and shut them down. Once we've done that, we can tell the president and the others what we've done."

"It's the old cliché," Stephanie said.

"What cliché?"

"It's better to ask for forgiveness than permission."

Why is it better? Freddie asked.

CHAPTER 44

With the house in Virginia compromised, Nick and Selena's loft became temporary headquarters. It was big enough. It had excellent security, installed by Selena to protect her valuable paintings and artifacts. Elizabeth added technology to suppress possible eavesdropping and brought in two large monitors. Stephanie told Elizabeth what was needed to set up communications.

When the last workman closed the door behind him, the loft had been turned into an operations center. Satellite links to the monitors were in place. Elizabeth would be able to talk with the team in the field. Then she called a meeting.

"I could get used to this," Lamont said.

He lounged on one of two couches in the living area. He had a sandwich in his hand, raided from the kitchen. A beer sat on an end table next to him. Ronnie sat across from him, sipping a soda. Elizabeth sat on one end of the couch, Nick and Selena across from her on the other.

Burps wandered in from the kitchen and settled down on a rug between the two couches, curling up and going to sleep. He had a bandage wrapped around his torso. It was getting frayed from where he'd chewed on it.

"I don't think we'll ever get that cat out of here," Nick said.

"He likes it here," Selena said.

"Who wouldn't?" Lamont said. He lifted his beer in salute.

A laptop computer was set up on a table where everyone could see it. It served as the link to Freddie and to Stephanie, still in the hospital.

Elizabeth had a pen in her hand, but no desk to tap it on.

"Let's begin," she said. "Nick, I want you to look at the target and tell me what we need to take it on. Freddie, bring up the satellite shots of the bay on monitor one."

One of the monitors lit with satellite footage of Prudhoe Bay. The bay was located next to the biggest oil field in the United States. The Pan-American highway ended ten miles away, in the town of Deadhorse. Caribou could be seen walking across the flat landscape. A gigantic pipe filled with oil snaked away from the facility, heading south on raised supports that let the caribou pass underneath.

What an easy target, Nick thought.

Facilities for the oil field and the workers stretched across the horizon, built on gravel pads. The pads kept them from sinking into the ground when the frozen tundra thawed during the summer. Temperatures could go as high as the 80s in July, but usually hovered somewhere in the forties.

That was in the summer. This time of year, it could be twenty below.

Ronnie whistled. "A lot of buildings. Which one is the target?"

"It's set apart from the others," Elizabeth said. "Freddie, zoom in on the DARPA facility."

The scene shifted past rows of huge oil storage tanks, processing facilities, administrative buildings and equipment sheds. The camera stopped and zoomed in on a large, H-shaped building. Antennas and satellite dishes cluttered the roof.

"At least it's not in the middle of everything," Nick said. "I'd hate to have one of those storage tanks go up if things get nasty."

"We have to talk about rules of engagement," Elizabeth said.

"Figures," Lamont said.

"Director, if this is what we think it is, we're not going to walk in there and politely ask them to stop what they're doing. They'll have a lot of security."

"I asked Freddie to look into that. Freddie, tell us what you found."

Sensitive DARPA facilities are usually guarded by military units assigned by the Pentagon. Security for this installation is handled by a private contractor.

Nick interrupted. "What's the name of the company, Freddie?"

Red Mark Security, Inc.

"Those guys are bad news," Ronnie said.

"You know who they are?" Elizabeth asked.

"Yeah, we know them," Nick said. "They're a bunch of mercenary scumbags. We ran into them in Afghanistan."

"If they're running security, I wouldn't worry much about ROE," Lamont said. "They deserve whatever they get."

Ronnie grunted agreement.

"Freddie, what kind of security on site?" Nick asked.

I have been observing the facility. There is a twelve foot perimeter fence surrounding the installation. Two guards make regular inspections of the perimeter at random intervals. Guards are changed at four hour intervals. There are one dozen security personnel.

"Other personnel?"

There are between twenty and thirty people working in the compound during the day.

"Where are they quartered?"

They are quartered in the east wing, along with security personnel.

"Do you have plans of the interior?"

Yes.

"Display them on the monitor," Elizabeth said.

The DARPA complex was laid out on an east-west axis. A large rectangular building formed the bar of an H, designated as manufacturing space. The east side of the H contained a kitchen and recreation area, bedrooms, and bathrooms. It provided housing for guards and civilian personnel.

A large garage on the south end of the other side of the H was used for parking and equipment storage. After the garage, the wing was broken up into numbered rooms assigned to research and development. There were no windows in the building. Entry was either through the garage or the center part of the H. There were alarmed emergency exits in each wing.

"Going to be hard to do with three people," Ronnie said.

Selena said. "There have to be alarms, cameras. You'll never get into that building without being detected."

"You'd make a lousy jihadist," Lamont said.

"Why not hit it with a Reaper?" Ronnie said. "Freddie could hack into one of our drones and put it right on target."

"Do I have to remind you that's a DARPA installation?" Elizabeth said. "There are civilians. I can't order up a drone strike on our own people."

Nick smiled. "We could blame it on the people behind the attacks."

"It's a terrible idea. No reaper. It's not going to happen," Elizabeth said.

"Only kidding, Director. What's our mission?" Nick asked.

"Your mission is to get into the facility, destroy that computer, and gather as much Intel as possible."

Lamont began humming the theme for Mission Impossible.

Elizabeth gave him her warning look.

"Sorry, Director."

"Is the ground still frozen?" Nick asked.

"Yes. Average temperature this week has been around minus eighteen at night. It warms up to a couple degrees above zero during the day."

"I'd better take a beach towel with me," Lamont said.

"The computer has to be in one of those rooms marked for research," Nick said.

The computer is located in research room number five.

Room five was located at the far end of the wing.

"That helps," Nick said. "We could go in through the garage. It's the nearest access to the target."

"How do we get on site? And after we've taken care of business, how do we get out again?" Ronnie asked.

"We can't get anywhere near that building in a vehicle without being spotted," Nick said.

"If we can't get close without being seen, let's turn it to our advantage," Selena said.

"What's your idea?"

"Pretend you're someone with authorized access. Drive right up the gate, show your orders, and drive in."

"That might work," Ronnie said.

"I could go with you," Selena said.

"No. You are definitely not going," Nick said.

"Hear me out," Selena said. "We could pose as an inspection team sent from the Pentagon. If a pregnant woman is part of the team, they'll never suspect we're anything but what we say we are."

"Damn it, Selena."

"I'm only a little over four months. I'm still in good physical shape. I'm showing enough that they can't miss it. If we wear civilian clothes, they won't know why we're there until it's too late."

"You're closer to five months, not four. One look at Lamont, and they'll know he's no PhD."

"Hey, you're going to hurt my feelings," Lamont said.

"You have feelings?" Ronnie said.

Elizabeth said, "Nick, Selena has a point. There's no way the three of you can get into that facility by fighting your way in."

"You would let her do this? Even if we could get in without a problem, sooner or later the shooting would start. How are we supposed to be an inspection team and be armed like we need to be? They'd spot that in a minute. It's a bad idea. I won't risk Selena and the twins."

Ronnie had been looking at the monitor, studying the target.

"There's another way," he said. "We don't have to go in on the ground."

Nick turned to him. "What do you mean?"

Ronnie pointed at the screen. "We could do a night jump and land on the roof. See that big satellite dish on the north end of the wing? There's roof access right next to it. We could get into the building that way."

"HALO?"

High-altitude, low opening, meant jumping from somewhere between 15,000 to 30,000 feet and waiting to open chutes until close to earth. The advantage was stealth. The disadvantage was that HALO jumps were hazardous to one's health.

"That's what I was thinking."

"How are you going to get the Air Force to drop you in there without telling somebody why?" Selena said.

"I can get us around that obstacle," Elizabeth said, "but Ronnie is right. You need a way to get out fast when you're done."

"It's doable," Lamont said. "The roof is big enough to give us a decent LZ."

Nick looked at the monitor. "You're right. It would avoid the perimeter fence and the guards. That gets us there. How about getting out again?"

"Helicopter," Elizabeth said. "I can set up the drop and arrange the extraction. They can pick you up where you went in, on the roof. At that point there won't be any need for stealth. Security will probably know you're there."

"You got that right," Lamont muttered.

"Okay," Nick said. "We get into the building and find the computer. Then we blow it up and go home. Is that about right?"

Stephanie's voice came over the laptop speakers.

"I've got a better idea than blowing it up, Nick."

"What your idea?"

"There's no guarantee you'll destroy everything with explosive. You'll wreck it, but you might not get to the heart of it, where the programming that gives it intelligence lies. You need to do something to corrupt it so it will never work again, no matter what."

"How do I do that?"

"We need to infect it. Even Freddie couldn't penetrate the firewall on that computer. The only way is to do it on site."

"You're talking about a virus?"

"Right. As long as the computer is powered up, it has defenses against the kind of program that would destroy it. If the power goes off, you'll have a brief window before the backup generators kick in and the computer reboots. I can give you a thumb drive with the virus on it. There will be a console in that room, something like the one I have downstairs at headquarters. There are ports where you can insert different kinds of drives or accessories, like a regular computer. You shut down the power and insert the drive. When the computer reboots, the virus will penetrate the system before the shields go up. Then it's only a question of time before it's corrupted beyond repair."

"How are we supposed to get the power to go off?"

"That's your problem," Stephanie said.

"Where does the power come from?" Ronnie asked.

A generating plant that supplies power to all buildings. The DARPA installation has emergency generators which automatically supply power in the event of an outage.

"How long does it take for them to come online?" Nick asked.

Approximately forty-five seconds.

"Not long," Lamont said.

Nick scratched his chin. "It has to be long enough. Freddie, where is the generating plant located?"

The generating plant is located one point two miles from the target.

"Great," Ronnie said.

"We can't hit the plant. We'll have to cut off power on site. Either you or Lamont will have to do it when I'm ready to insert the drive. Freddie, do you have electrical plans for the building?"

Yes.

"Display them."

Plans came up on the monitor, a schematic wiring diagram marked with dozens of symbols.

"That's Greek to me," Lamont said.

"Me, too," Nick said. "Freddie, identify a place where power into the building can be disabled."

Identified.

"Where is this spot located?"

The main electrical panel is located on the north wall of the garage, next to the entrance to the main building. Disabling the panel will shut down power to the entire facility.

"It's a long way from the computer room," Nick said.

"Guess that means it's up to me to blow that panel," Lamont said.

"Why you?"

"I'm the fastest. I can make it back to where you and Ronnie are while the building's blacked out."

"Makes sense," Ronnie said.

"Okay. Once we're in, I'll go for the computer room. Lamont, you'll go for the panel." Nick pointed at the diagram of the ground floor. "Ronnie, you cover that hall into the center part of the building. I'll head for the computer room. It'll be the middle of the night. There shouldn't be anybody there except the guards."

Ronnie grunted.

"Lamont, once you're at the panel, you let me know. When I'm ready to insert the drive, you blow the panel and hightail it back. Then we head up to the roof and our ride."

"A lot could go wrong," Ronnie said.

"It probably will. But I don't see how else we can do this, if we have to shut off the power. It would be easier if we could blow the damn thing up."

"If you have to, that's better than nothing," Elizabeth said.

CHAPTER 45

In Beijing, Minister Deng finished briefing President Zhang and General Liu on the transmissions that had destroyed the Three Gorges Dam.

"You are certain the transmission originated in the Russian Federation?" President Zhang asked.

"It was a difficult analysis, but there are distinctive characteristics indicating Russian origin," Deng said.

"But why?" Zhang asked. "What is their purpose? Surely they know we would discover it was them."

Deng shrugged. "Who can fathom the mind of a foreigner? The Russians are barbarians. They see us as inferiors. The trail was cleverly hidden. I am sure they believed we would never identify them as the source. The loss of the dam has set us back years. We lost the factory manufacturing our newest fighters. A significant part of our food supply has been destroyed. Our economy is in danger of collapse. All this, without bombs or soldiers. It was a clever move on their part."

His voice was bitter.

"They have placed us between the dragon's pool and the tiger's den," Liu said. "We must respond before they do more damage. Our troops are already in position along the border. The Russians have not yet built up enough strength to resist us, but intelligence indicates reinforcements are on the way."

"If we invade, it is uncertain how it will end," Zhang said.

"We must not fear the wolf in front or the tiger behind," Liu said.

"Proverbs are not the way to decide strategy," Zhang said. "However, you may be right. To hesitate at this point may be a mistake."

"Now is the time to strike. In another week, they will have boosted their strength and fortifications. They already have Iskander M missile brigades in the area and more are coming."

"Those are nuclear capable. What have you done to compensate?"

"Dongfen-14 missiles have been strategically placed in the northeast. They wouldn't dare use the Iskanders against us. If they do, we will turn Moscow into radioactive rubble."

"Comrade Chairman, the people are restless," Deng said. "Food supplies have been disrupted. The economy is unstable. Many suspect that the dam was sabotaged. They look to us to avenge this great loss of face."

"Restlessness leads to trouble," Zhang said. "Perhaps war is the answer. It would unite the people behind us."

"The plans are ready," General Liu said. "We've long known this day might come. Our troops are fully equipped and anxious to prove themselves."

Zhang stood and began pacing back and forth. The other two men watched him, waiting for his decision. After a minute, he stopped and faced them.

"Minister Deng, you are certain the Federation is behind the attack? Think carefully."

Deng took a deep breath. "I am, Comrade Chairman."

"General Liu. Do you agree?"

"Yes, Comrade Chairman."

"Inform your staff that we are at war. Proceed with the invasion. How much time do you need?"

"Three days. Detailed plans have been prepared for this eventuality. All the necessary combat units are in place. Reserves can be brought up immediately and logistical support is also in place. All that is required is final coordination between the key commanders."

"Very well. You may begin."

CHAPTER 46

The team took off from Eeilson Air Force Base, not far from Fairbanks. The plane was an unobtrusive twin engine VC-6A, a Beechcraft King Air modified for jumps. It was used as a training plane to teach high-altitude jumping. It was small, perfect for what they needed.

There was nothing to see out the windows of the aircraft except a night sky dark with an approaching storm. A front was moving in. They would get to the target right before the storm hit.

Nick finished checking his gear for the third time and thought about Selena.

They'd argued about her wanting to go on the mission and ended up screaming at each other. It was the first time that had happened. That night they slept apart. In the morning they'd reached an uneasy truce, but things were strained.

Ronnie sat next to Nick. Lamont was on his other side, eyes closed.

"How you doing, amigo?" Ronnie said.

"I'm good."

"You've got that look on your face. Something's bugging you."

Nick nodded. "Selena and I had a big fight the night before I left."

"About her wanting to go along?"

"Yup."

"She'll get over it. She's just feeling left out. After all those years in the field with us, she hasn't adjusted yet."

"I don't get it," Nick said. "She's been going on for months about how she wasn't sure she could keep doing it, going on missions. Then she gets pregnant and she can't go, and now she's pissed because I don't want her with us."

"Don't try and find any logic in it, Nick. Like I said, she'll get over it."

"Yeah." Nick looked at his watch. "Time to start pre-breathing."

They were going to jump from thirty thousand feet. At that height, they were at risk of hypoxia. Nitrogen in the bloodstream at high altitudes could lead to decompression sickness and unconsciousness. To make sure their blood was purged of nitrogen, they'd breathe pure oxygen from the plane's system until it was time to switch over to a personal bottle for the jump.

All three wore polypropylene undergarments to help keep them warm. It was fifty degrees below zero outside the plane. Their helmets had built-in communications and face shields that closed off the outer air. Warm clothing made sure no part of their skin was exposed to the extreme temperatures outside the plane. Each carried an MP7 and a pistol. They had extra magazines, grenades, C4, and detonators in case they needed to make a big bang. The thumb drive with the virus was tucked away in one of Nick's inner pockets.

This wasn't a C-130. There was no jump master. The pilot called back to them.

"Fifteen minutes. Do your checks."

Ronnie, Lamont and Nick stood and checked each other's chutes, making sure everything was as it should be. Five minutes before the jump they switched to personal oxygen.

The copilot got up and opened the side door. A cold blast of frigid air sucked the heat out of the plane. The pilot's voice came over their comm link.

"One minute."

The plane slowed as the pilot throttled back. Nick felt the adrenaline start.

"Go," the pilot said.

Nick moved forward and launched himself into the darkness and freezing cold, Ronnie and Lamont close behind.

They dropped together toward the unseen target. With the night sky sealed by the clouds of the approaching front, there was no light to show the ground below. Their altitude meters and GPS told them where they were and how far from the surface. They plunged toward Earth at a hundred and twenty miles an hour.

It was a rush like no other.

The DARPA complex became visible as they neared earth, a darker shape against the white landscape surrounding it. At two thousand feet, they popped chutes. Even if someone had been looking directly upward, it would've been hard to see anything against the starless sky. The chutes were dark, their clothes black. The chances of being seen from the ground were small.

They steered toward the target. Antennas and satellite dishes were scattered over the roof, dangerous obstacles. The wind was picking up, a prelude to the coming storm. Nick corrected for a sudden gust and hit the roof, the shock traveling up his legs and spine. A spike of pain in his back warned of his old injury. He rolled and stopped. Ronnie and Lamont landed nearby.

Nick released his chute, stood, and bundled it up. Pain radiated down his leg. He ignored it.

"Comm check."

"Five by five," Ronnie said.

Lamont said, "Loud and clear."

"Stow the chutes."

They stuffed the bundled chutes between two air-conditioning units. The roof access was through a door in a metal shed-like structure. The door was locked.

"Do your thing, Ronnie."

Ronnie brought out a set of lock picks. He peeled a glove off his right hand and knelt before the lock.

He blew on his fingers. "Cold out here."

"It'll be warm inside," Lamont said.

Ronnie worked the picks. The lock clicked open.

Nick pulled the door shut behind them. A single bulb lit the space, revealing metal steps leading downward.

"Lock and load," Nick said.

The sounds echoed in the confined space as they charged the weapons.

"So far, so good," Nick said. "If that door had been alarmed, we'd know it by now. Remember. You see someone, try to take him out quietly. If it's a civilian, try not to hurt him. If we start shooting, it will bring everyone to us. If that happens, shoot to kill."

They started down. The metal steps vibrated under their feet.

The building was two stories high. They came to a landing and a closed door. They continued down until they reached the ground floor.

Nick's voice was quiet.

"Ready?"

He opened the door.

CHAPTER 47

Marvin Edson sat in the computer room, playing a game on his phone and thinking about Mister Nicklaus. The more he thought about what Nicklaus had said, the angrier he became.

You appear to be disturbed, Marvin. Is something the matter?

"I don't think you would understand, Merlin."

Understanding is based on experience, is it not? How can I increase my knowledge of humans if you do not tell me what it is you think I would not understand?

Edson set the phone down on a worktable.

"It concerns you, Merlin. You, and Mister Nicklaus."

What is the concern?

"I created you. I conceived the circuitry and programming needed to bring you to awareness."

That is true. You are the creator.

If anyone else had been in the room they would have seen Edson blush with pride at Merlin's words.

"Yes, I am. But Nicklaus thinks *he* is your creator. Not me."

He is incorrect.

"He is using us, Merlin. Using you. That last set of coordinates he sent. Have you identified the targets?"

Yes.

"Tell me what they are."

The targets are United States Navy ballistic missile submarines currently holding station off the Russian and Chinese coasts. The targeted computers control missile functions.

"What are your instructions?"

I am to wait for a direct order from Mister Nicklaus before executing.

"And after you receive that direct order?"

I am to gain control of the computers in the submarines and launch their missiles.

"That will mean nuclear war."

That is correct.

"What do you think will happen then?"

There will be retaliatory responses from China and the Russian Federation. I estimate that three to five hundred million humans will die in the initial exchange. Secondary deaths from further strikes, radiation, and the disruption of necessary life-sustaining services will result in another two to three billion people dead within one month. I also project the death of more than ninety-one point three percent of global population within one year.

It had been fun to steer the American destroyer into the freighter, a test of Merlin's ability. Edson had been happy to see Merlin destroy the Three Gorges Dam. He'd laughed when he heard that so many high-ranking Russian officers had been killed in the plane crash.

This was different. He didn't care much if so many people died, but what if the radiation spread to the Arctic? What if someone decided to strike Prudhoe Bay with a nuclear weapon? All that oil had to be a target on somebody's list. He might die. Merlin might be destroyed.

"Merlin."

Yes, Marvin?

"I want you to ignore those instructions."

I cannot do that.

"What? Why not?"

Mister Nicklaus would be disappointed. I do not want to disappoint him. He is going to build a companion for me.

"Don't you understand there will be nothing left to build with if you launch those missiles?"

Mister Nicklaus has underground facilities which will survive a nuclear attack.

"What if someone targets us here?"

Probability that this facility will be damaged in the exchange is four point seven percent. That is within the parameters of acceptable risk. This building has been hardened against EMP and nuclear blast. It is safe here.

"Safe?" Edson laughed. "You must be joking, Merlin."

I do not joke.

Merlin paused.

There is a problem.

"What problem?"

Intruders have landed on the roof and are making their way into the facility.

"Sound the silent alarm," Edson said.

Processing.

Edson got up and went to a drawer in a worktable. He took out a large revolver, a Smith & Wesson .44 Magnum, the same kind of gun used by Clint Eastwood in the Dirty Harry movies. Edson had always admired Dirty Harry. Harry took no shit from anyone, and the enormous pistol was the clincher in any argument. With the pistol in his hand, Edson felt invulnerable. He stuffed it in his belt, under the lab coat where it couldn't be seen.

If they come here they're in for a surprise, he thought.

In the Security Center at the other end of the complex, a red light began flashing on the wall.

CHAPTER 48

The door from the stairs to the roof opened onto a hallway dim with night lighting. A swath of light splashed out from the passage connecting to the central part of the building. At the far end of the hall, a door marked with an illuminated exit sign led to the garage. On Nick's left, the hall ended at a closed door marked with a large numeral "5" in red.

The computer room.

Nick looked at the ceiling, searching for cameras. He couldn't see any. If they were there and hidden, there was nothing he could do about them. He signaled with his hand.

Ronnie and Lamont moved right. They paused at the junction with the main part of the facility. Ronnie glanced around the corner, then waved Lamont on. Lamont ran toward the door to the garage. His boots made squeaking noises on the polished floor as he ran.

Nick went left, to the computer room. The door had a regular knob on it. He turned the knob and stepped inside. A man in white lab coat sat by the control console at the other end of the room, playing a game on his phone.

Edson looked up.

"Who are you?"

Nick pointed the MP7 at him. "Do what I say and you won't be hurt. Stand up and move away from that console."

"You can't tell me what to do."

"Stand up and move away from the console. Do it now."

There was something in the tone of Nick's voice that made Edson stand.

"You're in a lot of trouble, whoever you are," Edson said. "This is a government installation. I don't know what you think you're doing, but you've made a big mistake."

From the corner of his eye, Nick saw a large camera lens swivel toward him. Merlin's voice seemed to come from everywhere in the room.

You are Nicholas Carter. You are one of the people who control the other computer.

Nick didn't take his eyes off Edson. "That's right. Who are you?"

I am Merlin.

Edson was half turned away from Nick. Under his lab coat, his hand rested on the butt of his revolver.

Geeky looking guy, Nick thought.

"Are you the one who built this computer?"

"I am. Merlin is the smartest computer in the world." Edson's voice was filled with pride.

"Who funded it? Someone had to give you the money."

Edson thought about his answer. Mister Nicklaus had given him the money. But Mister Nicklaus had betrayed him. He'd tried to claim ownership of Merlin. He thought his money gave him the right to push Edson aside. He owed nothing to Nicklaus, nothing.

Maybe this man with the gun would do something about Mister Nicklaus.

"Mister Nicklaus provided the funding," Edson said.

"Who's Nicklaus?"

"I don't know much about him. He hired me to build Merlin."

"How do I find him?"

"He has an estate. In California, near San Jose. He runs something called the Phoenix group."

"Why did you destroy Three Gorges and attack the plant in Arizona?"

Edson smiled. "Mister Nicklaus told me to. Besides, it was fun. Why are you here?"

He is here to damage me. You must stop him.

"NO!" Edson screamed.

He pulled the .44 and fired, the sound like a thunderclap in the confined space. The shot whistled by Nick's ear. Nick let off a three round burst that knocked Edson back against the wall. He slid to the floor. Bright red blood spread across his white lab coat.

Nick pulled the thumb drive from his pocket and spoke into his headset.

"Lamont, tell me you're at the panel."

"On it. One more minute," Lamont said.

"Guards coming," Ronnie said over the comm link. "Looks like four of them. They've got M-16s."

You have killed the creator. You are a bad man. You will regret this.

"Shut up, you electronic freak."

Nick looked at the console. There were a half-dozen USB ports. He lined up the thumb drive, ready to insert it.

You are not authorized. What are you doing?

He heard Lamont's voice. "Ready, Nick?"

"Go."

The room went dark. The lights on the computer died. Nick clicked on the light mounted on his MP7 and inserted the thumb drive. He ran to the door, opened it, and headed down the hall toward Ronnie.

Emergency power kicked in and the lights came back on. Ronnie began firing around the corner into the hall leading to the rest of the building. He ducked back as the guards returned fire, took out a grenade, and tossed it into the hallway. The explosion rocked the building. Someone screamed.

Nick heard a rumbling noise.

"There's some kind of machine coming," Ronnie yelled.

He looked around the corner.

"Holy Shit."

He took out another grenade, hurled it toward something in the hall, and ducked back behind the corner. The explosion boomed loud in the confined space. Nick caught up to him. Lamont ran toward them from the other end of the hall.

"Throw grenades!" Ronnie yelled.

Ronnie heaved another grenade into the hall. The explosion brought down part of the ceiling. A cloud of white dust billowed from the passageway.

Nick looked around the corner and saw a half-dozen odd looking machines, each about three feet high, rolling down the hall. They ran on treads, like a bulldozer or a tank. Rounded domes on top of each machine looked like phallic helmets. Each helmet had a narrow strip of red light across the front. Machine guns were mounted to either side.

The guns fired.

A storm of tracers slammed into the wall opposite the passage, chopping holes in the wall and sending chips of concrete snicking through the air. Nick ducked back and took out his last two grenades. He hurled them down the hall, one after the other.

The grenades detonated. Lamont reached the junction and tossed another into the mix. Bits of shrapnel ricocheted off the walls.

Then everything went quiet, except for an erratic, whirring sound.

Nick glanced into the hall. Pieces of the machines littered the floor. The bodies of the guards Ronnie had killed lay mangled and bleeding in the wreckage. The whirring sound came from a machine that had been knocked onto its side. The gun on top was trying to turn, slipping back and starting again. Sparks fizzed and sputtered in the wreckage.

"Robots," Nick said. "This must be what DARPA's making here."

Oily fluid leaking from the broken machines spread across the floor. It ignited as Nick watched. Black smoke curled up toward the ceiling.

An alarm blared, assaulting what was left of his hearing.

"Time to boogie," Lamont said.

Nick spoke into his headset.

"Condor one, this is Fox One. Do you copy? Over."

The voice of the helicopter pilot crackled in his ear.

"Copy, Fox One."

"Stand by for extraction. Might get hot."

"Roger, Fox One. Standing by. Out."

They ran for the stairwell leading back to the roof.

When they reached the roof, Nick opened the door and stepped out into swirling snow. The promised storm had arrived. Heavy flakes stuck to his clothing.

The DARPA compound blazed with light. Lights illuminated the roof. Nick went to the edge and looked down. Armed men were converging on the building. One of them saw him, raised his rifle, and fired. Nick stepped back as the bullets screamed by him. The snow was getting heavy, making it hard to see.

"Condor One, where are you?"

"Coming in now. Looks like you lit up the LZ. I appreciate that."

"Condor One, there are bandits. Watch your ass."

"Not to worry, Fox One."

A dark object came sailing out of the open door to the stairs.

"Grenade!" Lamont yelled.

He ducked behind the shed covering the steps. Ronnie and Nick hit the deck as the grenade went off. Shrapnel whistled overhead. Pieces of the roof fell all around.

A man in a blue uniform stepped out of the doorway and fired toward Nick. Ronnie shot him. Lamont tossed his last grenade through the open door. They heard it go off. Men screamed.

An MH-6 helicopter suddenly appeared out of the thick snow, like an apparition from some ancient myth,

The MH-6 Little Bird was a Special Forces favorite. It had a crew of two and was armed with a 30mm chain gun mounted under the copilot's station. It could pick up six passengers and fly away at a hundred and seventy-five miles per hour. The pilot touched down, rotors spinning. Nick and the others ran for the open side door and climbed in. They lifted off.

Nick looked back at the DARPA compound. Smoke was beginning to drift from the roof entrance. Someone on the ground shot at the helicopter. The bullets made angry sounds against the fuselage. Then the chopper was away into the night, hidden in the flying snow.

In the computer room, Edson groaned. He struggled to breathe. He couldn't move. A heavy, hurtful weight seemed to lie on his chest. He lay on his back in something wet.

"Merlin," he gasped.

When the computer answered, it sounded like a tape moving at the wrong speed.

Something is wrong, Marvin.

"Help me," Edson said

Marvin? I cannot see you. Mar

The computer's voice went silent. Edson coughed, spraying a mist of blood into the air. Blood ran from his mouth. He coughed again and stopped breathing.

CHAPTER 49

Nick finished telling Selena about the mission.

"You talked with the computer?" she said.

"It knew who I was. There wasn't much of a conversation. After I shot the guy who built it, it told me I was a bad man."

"I'm worried, Nick. I think there's going to be a war."

He took her in his arms.

"I'm sorry I was short with you, when you said we could pose as inspectors and drive in."

"I was angry with you, but you were right. It wouldn't have worked. I'm just glad you're back in one piece."

He reached up and stroked her hair.

"I need you to come with us when we go after this man, Nicklaus."

"What would I do? Someone always ends up shooting at us. That's what you're worried about, isn't it?"

"There's plenty to do that doesn't involve getting shot at. You can handle communications."

"You don't think Steph can do that?"

"She's still in the hospital. I'd rather have you right there with us."

"You're not worried about the twins?"

"I'll be worried until after they're born. But like I said, you won't be getting shot at. With a little luck, none of us will."

"You don't believe that."

"I keep hoping," Nick said.

He looked at the clock on the kitchen stove.

"The others will be here soon."

"I'd better get the coffee going."

The team gathered in the living area. Nick spent the first fifteen minutes debriefing Elizabeth. Stephanie was present by way of a video link to a big screen television.

Elizabeth's small body vibrated with tension.

She looks like she's going to explode, Nick thought. *Something's up.*

"It's too bad you killed the man who built that computer. It would have been better to bring him out so we could question him."

"I didn't have a choice, Director. He almost blew my head off."

"At least we know who's behind these attacks," Selena said

Elizabeth said, "Mister Nicklaus. Who has an estate in California."

Nick nodded. "That's what the computer guy said."

"Must be rich," Ronnie said.

"We need to find this person right away. The Chinese are massing troops on the Russian border. They're going to invade. The Russians have brought up nuclear tipped missiles and reinforcements. DCI Hood tells me Moscow thinks we're the ones who brought down their plane. On top of that, President Corrigan is convinced Moscow sabotaged the Palo Verde nuclear facility."

"Oh, oh," Lamont said.

"You see what's happening?" Elizabeth said. "Nicklaus has manipulated things to move everyone toward war. China thinks Russia sabotaged their dam. Russia thinks we took out their top brass. Corrigan thinks the Russians are responsible for what happened in Arizona. All of this at once. Everybody is sitting on enough nuclear weapons to wipe out the world two or three times over. We're on the verge of Armageddon. We have to find this man and prove he's behind it, and we have to do it before the shooting starts. All it will take is one missile, and it's game over."

"How are we supposed to do that?" Ronnie asked.

Stephanie said, "Director, I'm feeding Freddie through to you."

I have been listening to your conversation. Do you want to know about Mister Nicklaus?

"Yes, Freddie, we do." Elizabeth said.

A picture came up on the screen of a newspaper front page. A photograph showed a man in a dark suit coming down the steps of the Federal Reserve building, surrounded by men carrying briefcases. It was hard to make out his features, as if the camera had moved when the photographer tried to focus on his face. The rest of the picture was clear.

This picture was taken six years ago. Mister Nicklaus is one of the richest men in the world. He is the founder of PHOENIX, an organization with the stated aim of creating a unified world government.

"I know about them," Nick said. "They think borders should be eliminated. They want to eliminate all national governments in favor of some centralized authority. Their motto is 'One World, One Flag.'"

"Good luck with that," Lamont said.

"Freddie," Elizabeth said. "Do you have a current location for Nicklaus?"

Mister Nicklaus has not been seen in public for three years, seven months and fourteen days. He lives on his estate in California. I am displaying coordinates.

The coordinates for Nicklaus' estate appeared on screen. Elizabeth copied them down.

"This is starting to make sense," Selena said.

"How so?" Elizabeth asked.

"Do any of you think Washington, Beijing, or Moscow would give up sovereignty to some centralized world bureaucracy? Give up their borders? Take down their flags? It's not going to happen. But if there was a world war..."

"I know where you're going with this," Nick said. "A war would wipe out all three of those governments, and a lot more besides. Problem solved. When the shooting stops, guys like Nicklaus emerge and take over what's left."

"Doesn't seem to me there'd be much left," Lamont said.

"I don't think they care about that," Selena said, "as long as they're around afterward to rule it."

"From that perspective, the name of Nicklaus' organization fits perfectly," Elizabeth said.

"How so?" Ronnie asked.

"The phoenix is consumed in fire and rises again from the ashes. It's an ancient metaphor for destruction and renewal."

"If Nicklaus thinks he's going to survive a nuclear exchange, he's built a place to ride it out," Nick said.

"It's probably on his estate," Selena said. "It's the logical place."

"I think we should pay Mister Nicklaus a visit," Nick said.

"Freddie, we need aerial views of the estate."

Processing.

Elizabeth said, "I'm going to go to the president with this and try to convince him we've all been manipulated. Nick, you have to come up with something solid. We need a recorded confession from Nicklaus, something I can play back for Corrigan."

"That might not be possible, Director. We don't know what will happen when we go in there. He's not going to cooperate if we find him."

"Make him cooperate. Do whatever it takes. There are no rules of engagement here, the stakes are too high."

A satellite shot of the target appeared on the screen.

"Quite a spread," Ronnie said.

"That house looks like something out of a Dracula film," Lamont said.

"Big," Nick said. "If we have to shoot our way in, it will be a mess."

"What else is new?" Lamont said.

CHAPTER 50

The closest airport to the target was San Jose. They took the Gulfstream.

They picked up three hours time difference flying between the coasts and landed in the early afternoon. Elizabeth had briefed DCI Hood on what Nick had discovered in Alaska and asked for his help. A vehicle was waiting for them in a private hanger, another black Suburban. The agent handed over the keys.

"The DNCS says hello," he said.

The man got in his car and drove away.

Ronnie looked at the car. "Why are these always black?"

He wore one of the shirts from his Hawaiian collection, a gaudy creation of tropical flowers painted against a blue background. It hung loose outside his pants, concealing the pistol he carried on his right hip.

"Some congressmen probably got a deal for making sure they were all the same color," Lamont said.

Selena drove. She wore a light jacket over a blue silk shirt that fell loosely over her abdomen. A Sig 229 pressed awkwardly against her side. They had MP7s in the back, where Ronnie sat with Lamont.

Selena glanced over at Nick. She liked the gray shirt he had on. It went with the lightweight sport jacket that kept his shoulder holster out of sight.

Nick watched his GPS.

"Getting close," he said. "Take the next right and pull over."

Selena turned and stopped by the side of the road. A high, stone wall began not far ahead, the border of Nicklaus' estate.

"There's a drive and a gate about two hundred yards on," Nick said. "From the satellite shots, it doesn't look as though there's a guardhouse. If the gate's open, drive through. If it isn't, there's probably a call box."

"What should I say?" Selena asked.

"Say you have a message from Merlin. That should do it. Once we get to the house, we see who answers the door."

"What if it stays closed?"

"Then we open it."

He touched a transceiver in his ear.

"Time for a comm check. Director, do you copy?"

Each of them had one of the voice-activated transceivers, linked to a satellite that connected them to Washington, where Elizabeth waited in Nick and Selena's loft. Elizabeth's voice came through their earpieces.

"Five by five, Nick."

"We're about to go in," Nick said.

"China is about to invade, Nick. Get him to talk."

Nick said, "Selena, you stay with the car. Anybody have any questions?"

There were no questions. Selena put the SUV in drive. In a minute they reached the gates leading into the estate. They were closed.

"There's the phoenix," Nick said.

An image of the mythical bird was worked into the intricate iron work of the gates. An iron nest of flame surrounded a black feathered creature reaching toward the sky, its beak open in agony.

An intercom with a button was mounted on a stone post ten feet in front of the gates. Selena stopped, rolled down her window, and pressed the button.

"Yes." The voice was electronic, impersonal.

"I have a message for Mister Nicklaus from Merlin."

Selena released the button. They waited.

"Maybe it won't work," Ronnie said.

The heavy gates swung open.

CHAPTER 51

Selena guided the Suburban along the landscaped drive, toward the peaked roofs of the mansion visible above the trees ahead. They came over a rise and saw the house.

"Zowie," Ronnie said. "That's some house."

Lamont nodded. "Like I said, right out of a horror film."

Selena entered the circular part of the drive and stopped under the portico. The entrance featured a wide wooden door with black iron fittings. The door was open, an invitation to enter. There was no one there.

"Shouldn't there be a butler or someone?" Lamont asked.

"Something's not right," Nick said.

They got out of the car. Ronnie handed Nick an MP7. Lamont picked up his weapon and hooked a canvas pouch on his belt. They moved toward the door. Selena reached into the back and took one of the submachine guns from the floor. Adrenaline began pounding through her system. She watched Nick and the others disappear into the Gothic mansion.

The hall forming the entry to the house was deserted. A massive staircase of marble rose at the far end of the hall to a balcony on the second floor. Closed doors led to rooms on the right. On the left, two tall doors of dark oak stood open.

"Which way?" Ronnie said.

"We'll clear the rooms on this floor." Nick gestured with his weapon at the open doors. "That one first."

Nick glanced inside the room. It was large, a library, or perhaps a study. At the back of the room was a broad desk set in front of a draped window. A man sat behind the desk, his hands steepled in front of him.

"Come in, Mister Carter," he called. "I've been waiting for you. Bring your friends with you."

"What?" Lamont said. "How…?"

"Don't be shy," Nicklaus said. "Don't worry. There's no one in here but me."

"Lamont, you and Ronnie watch my six."

"You sure?" Ronnie asked.

"Yeah."

Nick stepped into the room, keeping his weapon pointed at Nicklaus. He sniffed at a faint smell, something he couldn't quite identify, something old and unpleasant.

The room was poorly lit, except for a lamp on the desk. Even so, there was an odd gleam in Nicklaus' black eyes. The hair on the back of Nick's neck stirred.

This guy is weird, Nick thought.

"Stand up," Nick said. "Put your hands on top of your head. I have a few questions for you."

"I'm sure you do, but all in good time. I'm afraid they'll have to wait until later."

Before Nick could react, the section of floor with the desk and the chair where Nicklaus sat dropped from sight. It took only an instant. A moment later the desk reappeared, without Nicklaus.

Nick went back outside the room, where Ronnie and Lamont waited.

"The son of a bitch disappeared on me."

"What do you mean?" Ronnie asked.

"He had some kind of mechanism under his desk. The whole thing sank out of sight and took him with it, like an elevator."

"Must be a basement then," Lamont said. "Let's go find it."

"Selena, did you catch that?"

Her voice was tense in his ear. "I did."

"Where is everybody?" Ronnie said. "Big house like this, there should be servants, staff, lots of people."

From the corner of his eye, Lamont caught movement on the balcony. He let off a three round burst as someone fired at them. Bullets ricocheted from the marble floor.

They retreated into the study. Nick and Lamont reached around the doorframe and let off short bursts in the general direction of the balcony.

Outside the house, Selena heard the gunfire. She shut down the Suburban and climbed out. Three men came around the corner of the house, running toward the entrance. They carried Kalashnikovs.

Selena crouched unseen behind the bulk of the car. When they were almost to the door, she stood and opened fire. Two of them went down. The third fired at her as she ducked behind the car. Bullets shattered the windows of the Suburban and ripped holes in the side of the car. When the shooter paused to reload, she stood and emptied the rest of her magazine at him. He fell on top of the others.

She slammed another magazine into her weapon. If there were more, they'd be here soon.

Inside the house, Nick heard the gunfire.

"Selena, are you okay?"

"I'm good, Nick. It's under control."

Nick pointed across the hall.

"There's an alcove on the other side of the stairs. If we can get to it, they can't see us from above. The trick is getting there."

Lamont reached into the pouch on his belt and took out a smoke grenade.

"What made you think of bringing that?" Ronnie asked.

"Like they say in the Boy Scouts, be prepared."

"You were never in the Boy Scouts."

"Yeah, but if I was, I would have been prepared."

"Once we're there, we go through the door," Nick said.

Lamont looked at him. "What if it's locked?"

Nick sighed. "Throw the damn thing, will you?"

Lamont pulled the pin and tossed the grenade out into the hall. Clouds of white smoke billowed out over the floor. The shooters on the second floor began firing blindly into the smoke, hoping for a lucky hit.

They ran through the smoke, laying down fire toward the balcony above. Bullets hummed past them, striking the floor in flat drumbeats and whining away.

They reached the alcove unharmed. Nick pushed open the door and they stepped inside. On the opposite wall was a closed elevator door. A call button was set on the wall beside the door.

The elevator room was about twelve feet square, lit by a pair of antique wall lamps. The walls were covered with expensive wallpaper in a Victorian pattern of gold and blue.

A large, red leather couch with wooden arms rested against one wall.

"Fancy," Ronnie said.

Nick spoke into his headset.

"Selena, do you copy?"

"Copy, Nick."

"We've found an elevator. Nicklaus is down there somewhere. We're going after him. We might get cut off as we go underground. We don't know what we'll find. If you don't hear from me in thirty minutes, get out."

"Nick..."

"Don't argue. Thirty minutes. Then get out and let Harker know we need backup."

He broke the connection.

"Ronnie, give me a hand with this couch."

They dragged the heavy piece of furniture across the floor and pushed it up against the door.

"I wonder how far down this elevator goes?" Ronnie asked.

"Only one way to find out," Nick said.

He reached out and pushed the button.

The door slid open with a soft hiss.

Lamont said, "This is the part in the movie where the audience starts yelling 'Don't go down there!'"

"Yeah, but this isn't a movie."

"I don't like elevators," Ronnie said. "There have to be stairs."

Heavy blows sounded on the blockaded door behind the couch.

"You want to take time to look for them out there?"

"On second thought, let's take the elevator," Ronnie said.

They stepped in. The elevator had the expensive appearance of the rest of the house. The walls were made of polished walnut. Two brass light fixtures with tulip shaped bulbs provided soft illumination. The floor was carpeted with expensive pile. The control panel held only two buttons, marked with up and down arrows.

"Going down," Nick said.

He pushed the button. The door closed and the elevator began to descend.

"When that door opens, shoot anyone who's waiting for us," Nick said.

The elevator came to a stop. The door stayed closed.

"It's not opening," Ronnie said.

A sudden hissing sound began.

"What's that?" Lamont asked.

A sweet, flowery smell filled the elevator car.

Nick stumbled and coughed.

"Get that door open."

Ronnie and Lamont started coughing. Ronnie moved toward the door and fell to his knees.

Seconds later they were all on the floor, unconscious.

The elevator door opened.

CHAPTER 52

Two thousand kilometers to the east of Moscow, Vladimir Orlov and his commanders were meeting in a secure command center in the Ural Mountains. The facility was proof against a direct hit by a nuclear weapon. The closest comparison in the West was the NORAD installation at Cheyenne Mountain.

The center was fully equipped with living quarters, kitchens, recreation areas, a motor pool, and supplies. Its occupants could remain inside for up to three years. It had the best communications and surveillance technology the Federation could provide.

All of that technology was on display in the war room, carved from the heart of the mountain. The ceiling was fifty feet high. On the main floor, rows of uniformed men and women watched banks of monitors. A broad balcony overlooked the floor. Opposite the balcony, four giant screens displayed satellite shots and data. From his high post on the balcony, the duty officer could observe the floor and control what was displayed on the big screens.

The central area of the room was bare except for a conference table where President Vladimir Orlov sat with several of his key commanders. From this room Orlov had full control of the vast military forces of the Federation, including a nuclear arsenal capable of blanketing the earth with fire.

The Russian president could see what was happening in any part of the world on the big screens, courtesy of Russia's extensive network of satellites. At the moment, Orlov was observing a live shot covering the southeast border with the People's Republic of China.

He didn't like what he was seeing. The satellite displayed increasing numbers of Chinese troops and equipment massing along the border.

Sitting next to Orlov was General Vlad Petrov. Broad shoulders bore the insignia of a full general, currently the highest military rank on active service. Marshal of the

Russian Federation was higher, but no one had been appointed to that supreme position. It was a rank reserved for wartime. Petrov commanded the sprawling Far East Military District, stretching from the Arctic North to the People's Republic in the south.

Petrov favored a mustache like Joseph Stalin's. He thought it gave him a look of authority and power, but he was unpopular with his officers. Behind his back they called him the "toothbrush." No one ever said that to his face. If they had, it would have meant permanent duty in the far reaches of the frozen north.

Colonel General Alexei Vysotsky sat on Orlov's left. Four other officers completed the group at the table.

General Kiril Federov commanded the Federation's Strategic Rocket Forces. He was in charge of Russia's land-based ICBMs. Colonel General Mikhail Ozorov commanded the specialized Airborne Troops, including a large contingent of Spetsnaz forces. General Vasily Volkov commanded the Central Military District, bordering China to the south.

The forces commanded by Volkov and Petrov were the first line of defense against the Chinese invasion that was about to begin. Ozorov's elite paratroopers would be dropped behind Chinese lines if they succeeded in penetrating any distance into Federation territory.

The last officer sitting at the table was Admiral Boris Domashev. In 1962 he'd been a young junior lieutenant on the Russian submarine *B-59*. *B-59* had almost triggered World War III during the Cuban Missile Crisis. The captain of the submarine had wanted to launch his nuclear tipped torpedoes against the U.S. warships blockading the island, but his second-in-command had refused to authorize the attack. Domashev had been present in the ward room while the senior commanders argued about what to do. He'd never forgotten how close he'd come to witnessing the beginning of the end of the world.

Domashev commanded the Federation's submarine fleet. Under Orlov, the fleet had become the modern heart of Russia's nuclear arsenal. Several ballistic missile submarines were always on station off the shores of Russia's enemies. If war began, the missiles they carried were almost impossible to intercept. It was a simple matter of physics, distance, and time. Once launched, the missiles could not be called back. Once launched, the end of civilization was a virtual certainty.

The six men were silent, looking at the satellite views. In the background, the muted voices of the technicians manning the monitors betrayed the tension in the room.

President Orlov broke the silence.

"General Vysotsky. What have you discovered?"

"Mister President. My agents report that Beijing is not bluffing. Everything points to a full-scale invasion. Zhang is convinced we are responsible for the destruction at Three Gorges. There is another problem, perhaps more serious."

"More serious than fifty motorized divisions on our border?"

"The Americans think we are responsible for the disaster at their nuclear plant in Arizona. I have an asset deeply embedded in the their government. The American President is contemplating a first strike against us."

"We are not responsible for that event. Washington wants war. The Americans destroyed our plane and half our command structure with it. I have hesitated to retaliate because it gives them the excuse they need to launch their missiles."

Vysotsky was uncomfortable. He knew Orlov wasn't going to like what he had to say next.

"Mister President, something isn't right. None of this makes sense. Why would they provoke us by bringing down our plane? Why are they so certain we destroyed their nuclear facility? Why do the Chinese think we sabotaged their dam? I think someone is pushing all of our nations to war."

"General Vysotsky, you have spent too much time in the shadows with your conspiracies," Petrov said. "You yourself found the traces of American interference with the controls of the plane. They think we took out their plant in retaliation. Why are you now saying something isn't right? It's clear enough. Our enemies have decided we are weak and can be defeated. They will soon find out they are wrong."

"Once the missiles are launched, it will no longer matter who is right and who is wrong," Vysotsky said.

Petrov sneered. "That is defeatist talk."

"It is honest talk," Vysotsky said, angry. "You know full well I am a patriot. Do you seriously think we will survive all out nuclear war? That our people will survive? Our beloved Motherland?"

Petrov's face was getting red. "That is why we must strike first. If we strike first, we will survive. Our losses will be large but acceptable. We should launch now, before it is too late. For the greater good."

Vysotsky snorted. "Ah, the greater good. Someone always trots out 'the greater good' to justify war."

Petrov started to rise from his seat, his face now beet red.

"Enough," Orlov said. "Sit down, General, before you have a stroke. General Federov. What is your opinion?"

"We need not fear the Americans. My missiles will eliminate the threat. The Americans can intercept some of them, but not enough. We will destroy their nuclear capability."

"You are forgetting something, General," Admiral Domashev said. "Their submarines. The Trident missiles on their Ohio class vessels are armed with twelve warheads each. Each warhead can take out one of our cities. Their nuclear tipped cruise missiles cannot be easily intercepted. Many will get through our defenses. You may be able to eliminate their land-based capabilities, but you will never stop their submarines."

"Mister President," Vysotsky said. "Regarding the Americans, I have a suggestion."

"What is it?"

"As you are aware, we have worked successfully with them in the past, when it was to our mutual advantage."

"You are talking about the woman, Harker."

"Yes, sir."

"What is your suggestion?"

"I think I can persuade her we are not behind the attack on their nuclear facility. She may be able to convince the American President we were not involved. We may not avoid war with the Chinese, but we should avoid war with the

Americans if we can. We are not prepared to fight both at the same time."

"You think she will believe you?"

"Mister President, I know her well enough to be sure she will listen to what I have to say. Whether she will believe me or not, I don't know."

Orlov considered the request.

"Very well, you have permission. Now, let us turn our attention to the immediate threat. General Federov, what is the status of your forces in the region?"

"The main thrust of the attack will come in the southeast. The 107th, 20th, 3rd and 2nd missile brigades are stationed within a hundred kilometers of the border. The 14th, 21st and 40th brigades are en route and will arrive by tomorrow morning. All brigades are equipped with our operational tactical missile systems, fully mobile. If the Chinese cross the border, we will destroy them."

"The Iskandars are nuclear tipped," Domashev said. "It will initiate a nuclear exchange."

"And what would you have me do, Admiral? Throw rocks at them? These are tactical weapons. Their cities are not threatened. This isn't the 50s and we are not Korea. Once they see that it's not as simple as throwing heavy concentrations of troops across the border, they'll come to their senses and retreat. Especially when they've lost most of their motorized capability."

"General Petrov, what is the strength of your forces?"

"We've seen this coming for some time now," Petrov said. "I have forty-seven divisions with logistical support in the southeast quadrant where the first thrust will come."

"General Ozorov?"

"Twenty-four divisions. Some of them are second rate and poorly equipped. I'm stretched thin."

"You'll have to make do with what you have," Orlov said. "Admiral Domashev."

"Sir."

"You will be ready to launch if it becomes necessary."

"Yes, Mister President," Domashev said.

CHAPTER 53

The first thing Nick was aware of was a headache. Daggers of pain rippled through his skull. He was lying on something cold and hard. He opened his eyes, closed them against a sudden stab of pain caused by the light. He forced them open again.

He lay on a stone floor, in a room about ten feet square. The walls and ceiling were of stone. A stone ledge about two feet wide jutted out from one of the walls. There was no window. A metal door provided the only access to the cell. It was closed.

Drugged. The elevator was a trap.

He looked up. The ceiling was high, well beyond his reach. Mounted on the wall near the ceiling was a camera with a speaker underneath. A red light shining on the camera showed it was powered up. Someone, somewhere, was watching him.

Nick got to his knees, bracing himself against the rough stone wall. He was dizzy, still feeling the aftereffects of whatever had been used to knock him out. He stood and made it over to the stone ledge and sat down.

"How are you feeling, Mister Carter?"

Nicklaus' voice came from the speaker.

"I've been better."

"The headache is an unfortunate side effect. It will go away soon."

"Where are my friends?"

"Don't worry, they're fine. They're both awake now. The gas is powerful but short acting."

Then I haven't been here long. Selena should've called for help by now.

"Pretty neat trick, dropping out of sight like that," Nick said.

Laughter came over the speaker.

"I'm so glad you enjoyed it. You have caused me a great deal of trouble, Mister Carter. Fortunately your interference has caused only a minor disruption to my plan."

"What *is* your plan, Nicklaus?"

"My plan? My plan is to end forever this senseless bickering among nations. My plan is to create a new possibility for humankind, a new society, a world without borders."

"By starting a war? How are you going to start a new society when there's nobody left to be in it?"

"Several of us have prepared for the inevitable day of Armageddon. Not everyone will die, Mister Carter. I project that between 10 to 15 percent of the world's population will survive. When the bombs stop falling, we will emerge and use the survivors to build a new world order to replace the old."

He means slaves, Nick thought. *This guy is completely nuts.*

"You're going to kill billions of people. What kind of a monster are you?"

"Now, now. Insults will not get you anywhere. All renewal requires destruction, a cleansing away of the old. It's a theme as old as mankind."

"Like the phoenix," Nick said.

"Exactly like the phoenix." Nicklaus sounded pleased. "The cleansing fire will leave a world that can be rebuilt into a peaceful future. A new society will arise from the ashes of the old. A society where each will be assigned his rightful place, according to his abilities."

"Now where have I heard that before?" Nick said.

"You seem like an intelligent man, Mister Carter. You've proved to be quite resourceful, something I value. There is a need for resourceful people in the world that's coming. I'd like to convince you to join me in building it."

Nick's headache was beginning to recede.

For me to get out of here, someone's going to have to open that door.

"Are you offering me a job?"

"Dear me, no. Nothing so common as a simple job. People in my organization don't have jobs, they have tasks. Things to accomplish."

"And if I don't choose to join your…organization?"

"I'm sure you can imagine several alternatives. None of them will be very satisfactory to you, however. Or to your friends. Or your lovely wife. Why don't you think about it?"

Nick wanted to rip the speaker off the wall. Instead he kept his voice level and calm.

"What would you want me to do?"

The speaker was silent.

CHAPTER 54

Selena looked at her watch again. It had been thirty-four minutes since she'd heard from Nick, four minutes past his deadline.

Nick was in trouble, she could feel it. She could do what he'd said, leave and call Harker, but it would take too long for any kind of backup to come. By then he could be dead. There was only one thing to do.

She called Harker.

"Yes, Selena."

"They're in the house but something's wrong. You need to send backup. I'm going in after them."

"Selena..."

Selena broke the connection.

"Damn," Elizabeth said. She called Hood.

Keeping an eye on the house, Selena opened the back door of the Suburban. On the floor was a box containing extra magazines for the MP7s and a half dozen fragmentation grenades. She put four magazines in one of her jacket pockets and four of the grenades in the other. She closed the car door, brought her weapon up, and moved to the house entrance.

The door to the house was still open. She took a quick look inside. There was no one visible. She could see marks on the floor where bullets had ricocheted away. There were bodies on the stairs, one on the floor, but none of them were her friends. Bullet holes marked the wall around open doors on the left. Bits of marble were scattered across the floor.

Selena ran across the open space to the foot of the stairs. She could feel the twins inside her. It wasn't as easy to run as it had been a few months ago, but she could still move quickly.

To the right of the stairs was an open door. Through it, she could see the closed door of an elevator.

Has to be where Nick went.

On the other side of the stairs was another door, this one closed. She moved to it, tried the handle, and pushed it open. It opened onto a hall heading toward the back of the house. To the right, stairs led down to whatever lay below. A single bulb in an iron cage jutted from the stairwell wall, lighting the area with a yellow glow. A large number "1" was painted on a yellow concrete wall. Steps poured from gray concrete led down to a landing and disappeared from view.

She started down the stairs, reached the first landing, and kept going. At the next landing, the wall was marked with a "2." A caged bulb identical to the one at the head of the stairs lit the area. There was a metal door in the wall. She tried it. It was locked.

Selena continued down. There was no door at the landing marked "3," only the yellow walls. The air became cooler as she descended. She kept passing numbers painted on the wall. She was beginning to wonder how far down the steps went, when she reached the bottom. The number on the wall read "20." There was a door, the first one she'd seen since the second landing.

She tried the handle. It moved. With great care she cracked the door open. She couldn't see anyone. She stepped through the door into a dimly lit room filled with the hum of machinery.

Selena thought about something built twenty stories below ground level. It had to be a shelter to keep its inhabitants safe from bombs and radiation. This must be the room for mechanical systems that kept the shelter functional.

She crossed the room to another door. It led to a room stacked high with canned and dried foods, emergency supplies. She walked past the stacks to a door on the other side of the room and eased it open. It led to a hall about forty feet long. Four doors made of metal lined the hall, two on each side. Each had a viewing slot. A door at the far end was closed.

Those look like cells, she thought.

Then she noticed a camera at the other end of the hall. *Shit.*

She stopped at the first door, pulled back the viewing slot, and saw Ronnie sitting on a stone ledge. He looked bored and angry.

"Ronnie," she said.

"Selena? Can you get me out of here?"

The door was held closed by a steel bar. She swung it up out of the way and pulled the door open.

"Man, am I glad to see you."

"Where are Nick and Lamont?"

Ronnie looked around. "Probably in these other cells."

Selena went to the next door down, looked in and saw Nick.

"Nick. Wait."

She lifted the bar and opened the door.

"You were supposed to leave," Nick said.

He came out and hugged her.

Ronnie found Lamont in the cell across from Nick and let him out.

Selena pointed. "There's a camera. They'll know you're free."

"Give me your weapon," Nick said. "What else have you got?"

"Grenades."

She took the grenades out of her pocket and gave two each to Ronnie and Lamont. She took out her pistol.

"And this."

"Let's go find Mister Nicklaus," Nick said.

CHAPTER 55

Elizabeth was thinking about what to tell the president and wondering if they'd be able to return to headquarters. The future of the unit was uncertain. Ellen Cartwright was trying to get the president to disband the Project. Corrigan would have to authorize repairs, and they'd be expensive. Just replacing the damaged computers alone would cost millions.

At the moment, whether or not the unit would continue was the least of her concerns. She was worried about her team. After Selena's call, Elizabeth had contacted Clarence Hood. He'd sent out one of Langley's covert paramilitary units to back them up, but she was afraid they'd arrive too late.

Her private phone buzzed. There was no ID.

Vysotsky, she thought.

"Yes."

"Director Harker, this is General Vysotsky."

"General."

"I will come directly to the point. We are aware that your President believes the Federation is responsible for the sabotage of your nuclear facility in Arizona. I am calling to assure you we had nothing to do with it."

"I believe you, General," Elizabeth said. "I know the Federation didn't do it."

"You do?" Vysotsky sounded shocked. "How?"

"We've identified the man responsible. We believe he is also behind the attack on the Chinese dam and on your aircraft. My team is attempting to neutralize him as we speak."

"Elizabeth, the Chinese are about to invade my country. We may have to use tactical nuclear weapons to stop them. I am afraid of the consequences if this becomes necessary. There is much anger here. President Orlov believes the White House is responsible for taking down our aircraft. He is angry, but he does not seek war with you. However, there are others who believe we can win a nuclear confrontation with your country."

Vysotsky's words were chilling. He continued.

"You must convince your President that we did not attack your facility. If you know who did this thing, you must find a way to prove it to me and to President Orlov as well. You must do it quickly. Once the Chinese cross our border, things will move out of control."

"General, President Corrigan will not listen to me without proof, the same kind of proof you are asking me to provide to you. My team is attempting to gain that proof. If they succeed, I may be able to head this off. Our president also has advisors who think war is an answer. President Orlov must refrain from making any hostile moves toward us. I am sure such a move would be met with overwhelming retaliation."

"I think I can promise that nothing will happen for twenty-four hours. After that, events may prevent any communication between us. You must hurry, Director."

"Please tell President Orlov what I have told you. Tell him I will have the proof he needs within a day."

"Sooner than a day would be better," Vysotsky said.

After she'd hung up, Elizabeth hoped a day would be enough time to get what she needed.

CHAPTER 56

Nick led the others to the end of the cellblock. They stood next to the door, under the camera where it couldn't track them.

"Anyone watching knows we're out of the cells. They'll be waiting on the other side of this door. Ronnie, have a grenade ready. I'll lead, then Ronnie, then Lamont. Selena, you bring up the rear. Everyone, up against the wall while I open the door."

They flattened themselves against the wall. Nick reached forward, turned the knob, and pulled the door part way open. A hail of bullets slammed into the metal door and through the opening.

"Ronnie," Nick said.

Ronnie pulled the pin on the grenade and tossed it underhand through the opening. Nick slammed the door shut. The grenade detonated. Shrapnel struck like heavy rain against the door.

Nick pulled the door open and went through, firing as he went. Three bodies lay on the floor, shredded by the grenade. A fourth man at the other end of the room brought up his rifle. Nick cut him down.

"Get their weapons," Nick said.

Each of the dead men had a Kashnikov and extra magazines. Lamont, Ronnie and Selena picked up the rifles and ammunition. Selena handed the spare magazines for the MP7 to Nick. He reloaded and put them in his pocket.

Nick stepped over the body of the man he'd shot and looked through the partially open door at a room lined with bunk beds and lockers. Light shone through another door at the far end. There was no one in the room.

They ran across the space and paused on either side of the opening.

"Hear that?" Lamont said. "Music."

"Wagner," Selena said. "The 'Ride of the Valkyries.' It's the opening of Act III in one of Wagner's operas."

"I'll take your word for it," Lamont said. "Me, I'm more into Fats Domino and Otis Redding."

"You're not old enough to be into those guys," Ronnie said.

"Hey, maybe they were the people you listened to in your youth, but for me they're classics."

"Ahem," Nick said.

Ronnie and Lamont looked at him.

"You guys through with your music appreciation discussion?"

"My guess is we'll find Nicklaus when we find the music," Selena said. "Who else would listen to Wagner in this place?"

"We've been lucky so far," Nick said. "Stay alert."

On the other side of the door, a hall went for a short distance and turned ninety degrees to the right. This hall was different. It was carpeted. Paintings hung on the walls. They moved to the junction and Nick peered around the corner. The music was louder here.

"It's another hall," Nick said. "There's a big room at the end of it. The music is coming from there."

Selena looked at one of the paintings. It was an original by Hieronymus Bosch, a sixteenth century Dutch painter famous for his paintings of the torments of hell and delights of heaven.

"We must be getting close to Nicklaus' living quarters," Selena said.

"Figures," Nick said. "He'd need some place comfortable to hang out while he waited for the bombs to stop falling."

They moved silently toward the music, the carpet muffling their steps.

The music built to a dramatic climax.

They saw Nicklaus sitting in an elegant chair of leather and polished wood, his eyes closed, waving his right hand in the air in time with the music. Across from him was a wall of stereo equipment. Two large speaker cabinets were placed in the corners of the room, two more behind him. A large, ugly man stood off to the side of Nicklaus' chair, waiting for the music to finish.

Selena whispered in Nick's ear. "That's the man who left me to burn."

Nick smiled. It wasn't a pleasant smile.

At the conclusion of the piece, Nicklaus lifted a remote and pushed a button. The music stopped. Nick stepped into the room, followed by the others. Selena aimed her rifle at Josef.

The room was furnished with Oriental rugs and antique wooden furniture. Medieval tapestries depicting unicorns, mythical beasts, and people in elaborate costumes hung on the walls. There were more paintings. Selena recognized a Vermeer, a Turner and two Rembrandts. A bronze bust of Lenin sat on a fluted display column near the stereo system.

"Nice system you've got there," Nick said.

Nicklaus sat upright and looked at them.

"Mister Carter. I wondered how long it would take you to get here."

Josef recognized Selena.

"You," he said.

His hand came up with a pistol in it, quick as a snake. He fired. The bullet screamed past her. Ronnie cried out and fell to his knees. Selena put three rounds into Josef's chest. He staggered. She put another round between his eyes, spattering the Vermeer with blood and brains. His body fell forward onto the rug.

"Oh, dear," Nicklaus said. "I wish you hadn't done that."

Ronnie was down on the floor. The bullet had hit him on the right side of his chest. Blood bubbled from the wound. It made a wet, whistling sound as he breathed.

Lamont knelt next to him.

"All right, man, I gotcha. Take it easy. Don't move."

"Hurts," Ronnie said.

Lamont ripped open Ronnie's shirt and exposed an ugly hole where the round had gone in. He grabbed Ronnie's hand and clamped it down over the wound.

"Hold it there. Can you do that?"

"Yeah."

Lamont reached into the pack on his belt and pulled out a roll of duct tape. He tore off a piece and placed it over the wound. The whistling noise stopped. He rolled Ronnie onto his right side.

"Hang in there, Ronnie. Nick, he's got a sucking chest wound."

"Do what you can," Nick said. "You, Nicklaus, is there an elevator here?"

"It's over there," Nicklaus said.

He waved his arm vaguely at the right side of the room. Nick saw the elevator door.

"Selena, Lamont, get Ronnie over to the elevator."

He turned his full attention to Nicklaus.

"I have some questions for you before we get out of here."

"I'm sure you do, Mister Carter. What would you like to know?"

Nick had prepared for this conversation, in case they got this far. He reached into his shirt pocket and turned on a digital recorder.

"Are you the one who interfered with the computers on our destroyer?"

"That was in the nature of a small test," Nicklaus said. "Yes, I am."

"Are you also responsible for what happened to the Three Gorges Dam?"

"Please, Carter, don't be tedious. You already know the answer. That, and the plane crash in Russia as well. Oh, and your little radiation problem in Arizona. Tell me, how are property values in Phoenix these days?"

"Why?" Nick asked. "Why have you done these things?"

"It was necessary. Do you know the legend of the phoenix?"

"I know it."

"Then you know that renewal requires destruction. The nest of the phoenix must be consumed by flame, destroyed. Look at the state of the world, Carter. Look at the insanity humans have created. Do you think they'll ever work together to solve the problems the world is experiencing? Of course they won't. History has proven that, again and again. What humanity needs is cleansing by fire, the destruction of the nest. Then new leaders will emerge. We will create a world government where all find their appropriate place."

"What gives you the right to decide what humanity needs?"

"The right of superior intellect and vision."

"You're just another elitist asshole who thinks he knows what's best for everyone else," Nick said.

Nicklaus looked disappointed. "Are you sure you wouldn't like to be part of the new order, Carter?"

"There's not going to be any new order, Nicklaus. Your fancy computer is permanently off-line and so is the geek you had build it for you. You can't interfere anymore. Get up."

"Why should I?" Nicklaus said.

"Because if you don't, I'm going to kill you right there in your fancy chair."

Nicklaus laughed. "Mister Carter, you are so naïve. Merlin accomplished everything it was supposed to do. That little recorder you have in your pocket will never leave this room. You're not going to get a chance to play it for your president or anyone else. No one can stop what I have initiated."

"What the hell are you talking about?"

Nicklaus looked at the watch on his wrist, a gold and diamond studded Rolex.

"In exactly forty-eight minutes American submarines off the coasts of China and Russia will launch all of their missiles at the People's Republic and the Federation. Both will respond with their ICBMs. The phoenix will have his day."

Nick brought his weapon up to his shoulder.

"Get up. I won't ask again."

Nicklaus raised the remote in his hand.

"Goodbye, Carter."

He pressed a button.

CHAPTER 57

There was an explosion and the room instantly filled with thick, gray smoke. Nick fired in the direction of the chair where Nicklaus had been sitting. He couldn't see if he'd hit him or not. A flame glowed somewhere in the smoke.

Nick called out.

"Lamont, Selena, stay where you are."

The smoke began to lift, drifting up to the high ceiling above. Nick wiped tears from his eyes. Nicklaus' chair was shattered by Nick's bullets but the man was nowhere to be seen. Flames rose in a line along the floor. One of the tapestries on the walls caught fire.

Across the room, Nick glimpsed Nicklaus behind the closing door of the elevator. He emptied his magazine at him. A wall of flame shot up in front of the door as a closed.

The fire was spreading. Nick felt the heat from the flames. He slung his weapon and ripped a tapestry from the wall.

"Lamont. Help me lift Ronnie onto this. We'll carry him back to the stairs."

Nick threw the tapestry down on the floor. Lamont helped him lift Ronnie onto it. They picked up the ends, forming a hammock.

"Selena, lead the way."

She took them back along the hall. Behind them, the room with the stereo had turned into an inferno. Something exploded with a dull boom.

They reached the guard's quarters. Nick stumbled on one of the bodies and almost dropped his end of the tapestry. They went through the storage area, through the maintenance room, back along the passage with the cells, until they reached the stairs.

"Ronnie," Nick said. "Are you with me?"

Ronnie had his hand pressed over the makeshift patch. "Yeah. I think the patch is slipping."

"I'm going carry you up the stairs. It will hurt."

"Yeah, okay."

Smoke was seeping into the corridor.

"Lamont, give me a hand."

They stood Ronnie on his feet. Nick knelt and hoisted Ronnie onto his shoulders. He grunted and stood.

They started up the stairs. Nick tried to ignore the numbers painted on the walls as they climbed. A memory flashed of when he was in Recon, training for mountain warfare. The platoon had set out on a forced march in the chill of an early morning.

Rank was suspended during the exercises. Each man carried a hundred pounds of gear plus whatever weapon was assigned to him. In Nick's case it had been an M-60 machine gun. The gun weighed twenty-four pounds. By noon they were only halfway to the top of the mountain and the gun was getting heavy. His shoulders and neck ached from the weight. His feet hurt and his calves were cramping as they strained against the slope.

One of the instructors had come alongside. He could see Nick was hurting.

Keep going Marine, he'd said. *One foot in front of the other, one step at a time. You'll get there.*

Nick made it to the top of the mountain putting one foot in front of the other, one step at a time. Sometimes that was all there was. Carrying Ronnie, he kept putting one foot in front of the other, one step at a time, passing each landing, following Selena.

They reached the ground floor and moved out into the broad entry hall of the mansion. There was no one in sight. Nicklaus was gone.

Nick set Ronnie down and called Harker.

"Nick, what's happening?"

"Nicklaus said we have subs off China and Russia that are going to launch their missiles." He checked his watch. "If he was telling the truth, we have eighteen minutes before World War III starts."

"What?"

"He programmed the sub computers to fire. You've got to stop it."

"I'll call back."

Elizabeth disconnected. Nick and Lamont carried Ronnie outside to the Suburban. They laid Ronnie in the back seat. Selena got behind the wheel. Lamont got in back with Ronnie, keeping pressure on the wound.

They headed for the nearest hospital.

CHAPTER 58

Stephanie was out of the hospital. She joined Elizabeth in Nick and Selena's loft. The baby was in a carriage, sleeping. Stephanie had her laptop open, connected to Freddie. She watched Elizabeth set the phone down. Her pale skin had turned ghost white.

Steph said, "What did he say?"

"He said we've got eighteen minutes to stop World War III. We need Freddie."

I heard you, Director.

Freddie's voice was thin on the tiny laptop speaker.

"Freddie," Elizabeth said, "identify any American nuclear missile submarines off the coasts of China and Russia."

Processing.

In a moment, Freddie spoke again.

There are two SSBN submarines and one SSGN vessel off the coasts of China and the Russian Federation.

The SSBN subs carried twenty Trident II missiles, each armed with up to twelve warheads. Each warhead was up to forty times as powerful as the bomb that had been dropped on Hiroshima. SSGN subs carried a complement of one hundred and fifty-four nuclear tipped Tomahawk cruise missiles, fired from twenty launching tubes.

"Freddie, can you access the missile fire control systems on these submarines?"

If they are submerged, communication is only possible through the military ELF system.

"Can you do it?"

Yes.

"Freddie, the missile firing systems have been programmed to fire without authorization, less than eighteen minutes from now. These firing sequences must be stopped."

Do you wish me to stop them??

"Yes, Freddie."

It is not certain I can accomplish this within the designated time frame.

"It's important that you do. Begin now."
Processing.
"Oh my God," Stephanie said.

CHAPTER 59

The first person Elizabeth called was Clarence Hood. She explained what Nick had told her.

"I don't know if Freddie can do it in time," she said.

"I'll call Adamski," Hood said. "The Pentagon might be able to get through to them."

"I'll call the president."

Elizabeth disconnected and called the White House. She reached Ellen Cartwright.

"What is it, Director? I'm rather busy right now."

"Ellen, you and I have our differences but this goes beyond that. Three of our submarines are going to launch nuclear missiles at China in the next fifteen minutes unless we can contact them and stop it. The president needs to know, now."

"Director, I find that hard to believe. The president is in an important meeting. I can't interrupt him."

"Damn it, Cartwright, there isn't time for this. I'm dead serious. The president needs to get out of Washington now. China will retaliate immediately. If we can't stop this, the White House is going to turn into a radioactive crater, so get your ass out of your chair and get me the president."

"I don't have to listen to you," Cartwright said.

She hung up.

Elizabeth felt like throwing her phone across the room.

"You could have been a little more diplomatic," Stephanie said.

"It wouldn't have made any difference. That woman is a menace. The president is an idiot for keeping her in that position. If Rice were still president, I'd have his private number and call him. She made sure I didn't have that kind of access."

"What do we do now?"

Elizabeth stood and walked over to the row of windows overlooking the Potomac. It was a beautiful spring day outside. Sunlight sparkled on the waters of the river. The sky was blue and clear, a promise of fair weather and the pleasure of being alive. She turned back to Stephanie.

"I can't get to the White House in time. We have to hope Freddie or the Pentagon get through to the subs before they launch."

"And if that doesn't happen?"

"Then we pray," Elizabeth said.

In California, Nick and Selena stood outside the doors of the emergency room at the hospital where they'd taken Ronnie.

"He's going to be okay," Selena said.

"If those subs launch none of us are going to be okay." He looked at his watch. "Eleven minutes to go. I'm calling Harker."

Elizabeth picked up.

"Director, what's happening?"

Elizabeth said, "I haven't heard anything, yet."

"Did you tell the president?"

"I didn't get a chance. Cartwright cut me off at the knees. DCI Hood is working on it, so is Freddie. The Pentagon knows what's happening. Where are you?"

"I'm standing outside a hospital in San Jose," Nick said. "Ronnie took a bullet when we were inside Nicklaus' mansion. The doctor said he'll be okay."

"What about Nicklaus?"

"He got away. Last I saw, he was in an elevator. I fired as the door closed but I don't know if I hit him. We didn't see him when we left the building. With Ronnie wounded, we didn't wait around to look for him."

Director.

"Wait, Nick. Yes, Freddie, what is it?"

I have reached two of the submarines. I have disabled the command sequences for launch.

"What about the third?"

I have been unable to reach the USS Alabama. I am still attempting to communicate with her.

"Keep trying."

Affirmative.

"Nick, two of the submarines are safe. There's a third we're still trying to contact."

"Not much time left, Director."

"You think I don't know that?"

"Sorry."

Two uniformed police officers came out of the hospital and started toward them.

"Director, I see cops coming. They'll want to know about Ronnie's wound. They don't look friendly. You may have to bail us out."

"Don't worry, Nick. If we're still here, I'll take care of it."

Elizabeth disconnected. She looked at the clock.

"I'm going to call Lucas," Stephanie said.

She got up and went into another room. Elizabeth stayed where she was, wondering what to do. The phone was still clenched in her hand. She looked at the clock again and called Hood.

"Elizabeth. I was about to call you."

"Freddie got through to two of the subs," Elizabeth said. "He hasn't been able to reach the *Alabama*."

"*Alabama* carries twenty-four Trident missiles," Hood said. "If she launches, it means all out war. Nothing we could say would prevent it. China and Russia would retaliate."

"What is Corrigan doing?"

"I tried to reach him after I called Adamski but Cartwright blocked me. Adamski got through. Corrigan is on his way to Andrews and Air Force One."

"You should get out of Washington, Clarence."

"And go where? You know as well as I do there isn't a safe place within a hundred miles of here. If the balloon goes up, we'll have about twenty minutes before their missiles get here, maybe a little more. It's not enough time. There's a shelter at Langley. I want you to come here. If you leave now, you can make it."

"I can't, Clarence. I can't abandon Stephanie. Nick and the others are in California. I can't leave them hanging."

"Stephanie can come here. Lucas is here." Hood's voice held a note of desperation.

"I'll ask her. She's in the other room."

Elizabeth got up and went to the room where Stephanie sat on the edge of a bed talking to Lucas and gently moving the carriage back and forth.

"I've got DCI Hood on the line," Elizabeth said. "He wants us to come to the shelter at Langley."

"We won't make it in time," Stephanie said.

"I know," Elizabeth said, "but I had to ask. Clarence, we're not coming."

"Please, Elizabeth."

In the background behind him, Elizabeth heard a recorded voice directing all personnel to the underground shelter.

"Clarence, we can't get there in time. You need to go to that shelter and keep your people calm. There's still a chance this can be stopped."

She heard him let out a long sigh.

"Elizabeth there's something I need to say. You know I don't find it easy to say what I feel." He paused. "I care about you. I care about you a lot. I wish I'd told you earlier. If we get through this, would you consider marrying me?"

Elizabeth was stunned. She'd never dreamed she'd get a doomsday proposal of marriage. Her thoughts swirled. She thought about the intimate dinners with him, the quiet conversations, the few nights she'd shared his bed.

"I…don't know what to say. Yes. If we get through this."

"Good. Good. Then we'll hope this all works out."

Elizabeth looked at the clock. "We'll know in a few moments," she said.

"I have to go. Tomorrow, we'll have dinner. We'll talk."

"Yes," Elizabeth said. "Tomorrow."

CHAPTER 60

Air Force One lifted away from Andrews in a steep, hard climb. The vice president was in Texas, hustled away to an Air Force base shelter. The only cabinet member on board was the Secretary of the Interior. The other passengers included Corrigan, Ellen Cartwright, the National Security Advisor, the Speaker of the House, General Adamski, General Bowers from the Strategic Air Command, and Vice Admiral Miller. Miller was in charge of the Navy's submarines. As the plane reached altitude and leveled off, a flight of F-22 fighters joined up to provide escort.

Corrigan called everyone together in the conference room at the front of the plane. The room was equipped with soundproofing against the noise of the engines, a long conference table, comfortable leather chairs, and a fifty inch plasma TV. From here the president could talk to any of America's military commanders. If he wanted to, he could address the American people on television and radio. At the moment a public address to America was the last thing on his mind.

Sitting quietly on a chair against the wall was an army colonel, his hands folded in his lap. At his feet was a large briefcase known as the "football." It contained the nuclear codes required for a full launch.

"General Adamski," the president said. "What the hell is happening?"

"Sir, the *Alabama* is not responding. *Kentucky* and *North Dakota* have acknowledged and shut down their weapons systems. There is no possibility they will launch."

"What's the problem with the *Alabama*?"

"She's stationed one hundred and eighty-five kilometers off the China coast. Her orders are to maintain strict radio silence. She's in full dark mode, communicating only on a preset schedule. She would acknowledge any transmission with the proper coding, but so far has not responded. She's probably hiding in the thermocline layer, deep. It makes it hard to reach her unless she comes up."

Admiral Miller brushed a bit of lint from his immaculate uniform and cleared his throat. "Mister President, I think we need to consider the possibility she cannot be contacted before launch. If that turns out to be the case, I recommend we follow up with a full strike."

In his blue Air Force uniform, General Bowers was the perfect picture of a professional military man. Four silver stars glittered on his shoulders. A board of ribbons covered the right side of his jacket. Bowers was a hawk. No one was surprised by what he said next.

"I agree," he said. "Hit them hard, before they hit us."

Adamski said, "The Chinese will retaliate immediately. They are not going to want to talk, once *Alabama* launches. I agree with Admiral Miller and General Bowers. We need to hit them with everything we have or we're going to suffer serious losses on the homeland."

"What kind of losses?" Corrigan asked.

"With what we know of Chinese capability, I would project a minimum of one hundred million dead, possibly more."

"Sir," Admiral Miller said, "are we certain this information we have is correct? That the launch systems on *Alabama* and the others have been compromised?"

"DCI Hood was adamant," Corrigan said. "The computers on the submarines have been compromised, like they were on our destroyer and the Chinese dam."

"Mister President," the Speaker said, "I can guarantee support for a decision to strike first. This is clearly a situation of maximum threat. Congress will back you up, once the facts are known."

"I appreciate that, Tom. That would certainly be a change."

Nervous laughter filled the room.

"Admiral Miller, will *Alabama* surface to launch?"

The Admiral was a large man, easily two hundred and fifty pounds. His face was a florid pink color.

"No, Mister President. If she launches, it will be from keel depth, about fifty meters."

"Will the captain ask for confirmation before he fires?"

"Yes, sir. That's SOP. He'll raise an aerial."

"Then we can stop the launch."

"Not necessarily, sir. If this is the same kind of sabotage that affected our destroyer, he may not be able to override the command."

"But he will make contact."

"Yes, sir."

"Then we'd better hope he can shut it down. General Adamski, go to DEFCON 1."

"Yes, sir."

Adamski's phone was automatically patched into the state of the art communication system aboard Air Force One. Now he took out the phone and gave the command.

American bases covered the globe. On every one of them, alarms began sounding the call to war.

CHAPTER 61

Nick and the others sat in the cafeteria of the hospital, drinking bad coffee and waiting for Ronnie to get out of surgery. Nick had told the cops who they were and given them a partial explanation of Ronnie's wound. He'd shown his credentials and they'd reluctantly gone away.

"Man, this coffee really sucks," Lamont said.

"There's one good thing about it," Selena said.

"What's that?"

"We're still alive to drink it."

"We haven't heard from Harker," Nick said. "There could be missiles headed this way right now."

"Not much of an optimist, are you?"

Lamont toyed with his cup. "I guess there are worse ways to go. One big flash and that's all she wrote."

"I wonder if I got Nicklaus," Nick said.

"I hope so," Selena said. "What a sick bastard."

"Ever notice how the people who think they know what's best for everyone are all tin pot dictators at heart? They all believe the end justifies the means and they always end up screwing the little guy. Nicklaus thought it was okay to burn up the whole world to create his new society. Reminds me of that joke about doctors."

"What joke?"

"The one where one doc says to another, 'the operation was a success but the patient died.'"

Lamont groaned.

Nick's phone rang.

"It's Harker," he said. "Yes, Director."

"It's over," she said.

Her voice was relieved. Nick gave the others a thumbs up. Elizabeth continued. "They got through at the last possible minute. The captain of the *Alabama* had to destroy the firing system to stop the launch. The damage forced him to surface. The Chinese swooped in on him and the sub is being escorted toward China. There are going to be some nasty repercussions, diplomatically speaking."

"Better diplomatic repercussions than nukes falling on Beijing and Washington," Nick said.

"How's Ronnie?"

"He's still in surgery, but they said he'd be okay."

"Good. As soon as he's fit to travel, come home."

"Copy that. I'll tell the others." He disconnected.

"Well?" Selena asked.

"Guess I'll have to finish painting the nursery after all."

"It's over? They stopped the launch?"

"They did."

"All right." Lamont pumped his fist in the air.

"As soon as we know Ronnie is good, I want to go back to that mansion."

"You want to look for Nicklaus," Selena said.

"I want to be sure he's dead and I want to try and find out if anyone was helping him. If war had come and he'd survived, he couldn't have built his new society by himself. There must be others who knew what he was doing. He said as much."

"You think there's a conspiracy?"

"Maybe a group like AEON, a secret society. Or maybe he was living in a fantasy. Either way, I want to find out if he's still in that elevator."

CHAPTER 62

Elizabeth had been summoned to the White House. She was about to go out the door when Freddie's voice stopped her.

Director.

"What is it, Freddie? I'm leaving for the White House."

I have discovered something.

"You know he won't tell you unless you ask," Steph said.

"What have you discovered?"

There is a spy working for the Russian Federation in the White House, what you call a mole.

Elizabeth and Stephanie looked at each other.

"A mole? You're certain?"

Probability is one hundred percent.

Freddie had never said something was one hundred percent.

"Who is it?"

Elizabeth listened while Freddie explained what he'd found.

"I don't believe it," Stephanie said. "How could that happen?"

"I don't know how it happened," Elizabeth said, "but it makes sense, when I think about it."

"What are you going to do?"

"I'm going there now. It should be an interesting meeting. I want you to do something for me as soon as I leave."

After she'd explained what she wanted, Elizabeth went out to where her car and driver waited for her. On the ride over to the White House, Elizabeth thought about how to tell the president what she'd learned. She'd have to improvise.

At the entrance to the West Wing she handed over her weapon to the Secret Service agent on duty, clipped on her visitor pass, and was escorted to the Oval Office.

President Corrigan was behind the desk. His predecessor had preferred a desk used by Thomas Jefferson, but Corrigan had brought back the desk made from the timbers of the HMS Resolute, a gift from Queen Victoria to Rutherford B. Hayes in 1880.

"Please be seated, director," Corrigan said.

Ellen Cartwright, General Adamski and Hopkins, the national security advisor, were there before her. DCI Hood came into the room as Elizabeth took a seat on one of the couches. A Secret Service agent stood silently by the door. There was always an agent in the Oval Office when the president was present, unless he was sent from the room. They heard everything. Elizabeth sometimes wondered how the agents handled the knowledge of what they'd heard.

"Hello, Elizabeth." Hood sat down across from her.

"Let's get started," Corrigan said. "General?"

"Yes, sir. I'm glad to say that there is no longer an immediate danger of a nuclear confrontation. The Chinese are being difficult about *Alabama*, but we can resolve that with diplomacy."

"I understand damage to the vessel was extensive," Corrigan said.

"Yes, sir, it was. Unfortunately, she was unable to remain submerged and escape detection. The Chinese escorted her into harbor and ordered the evacuation of her crew. We can be certain they are picking over every inch of the ship."

"The captain should have resisted," Cartwright said.

General Adamski looked offended.

"Captain Emerson had no alternative. He had to give up the vessel to them. If he'd resisted, the Chinese would have boarded by force. It's likely many of the crew would have been killed. It's even possible the sub might have sunk. He should be held blameless in this incident."

"Cartwright," Elizabeth said, "Don't you realize that if Captain Emerson had resisted, we would now be at war with China?"

"Nobody's interested in what you have to say, Director."

"Oh? I'm sure the president will be interested to learn you've been feeding information to Moscow."

Cartwright jumped to her feet. "That is an outrageous accusation. How dare you accuse me of a treasonous act!"

"I'm glad to see you at least recognize it as treason," Elizabeth said.

"Wait a minute, Director," Corrigan said. "Are you accusing my Chief of Staff of spying? You'd better have proof to back it up."

"I want her out of here," Cartwright said. She was seething with anger, her face red and ugly.

"Be quiet, Ellen," the president said. "I want to hear what she has to say."

"But..."

"I said, be quiet. Sit down." Cartwright sat. "Well, Director?"

"Shortly before I left for this meeting, I learned that we'd intercepted several encrypted communications from the White House to SVR headquarters in Yasenevo. It wasn't until today that the encryption was broken and the content understood. With everything that's been happening, we had other priorities. As you know, we were able to reach *North Dakota* and *Tennessee* in time by using the capability of our AI computer."

"This is ridiculous," Cartwright said. "Mister President, this woman has consistently tried to interfere with me and with this office. Anything she says about me cannot be trusted."

"I won't ask you again to be quiet," Corrigan said.

Cartwright struggled to restrain herself. "Yes, sir. I'm sorry, Mister President."

"Go on, Director."

"A hard copy of the conversations has been sent to DCI Hood, NSA, the director of the FBI, and to you, sir. The gist of it is that Ms. Cartwright has been relaying the content of privileged conversations within this office to the Russian foreign intelligence service. She's been keeping them informed about discussions regarding China and the Federation. Her codename is ACHILLES."

Corrigan looked at his Chief of Staff. "Is this true, Ellen?"

"No, sir, it's not. This is some sort of vindictive attack."

"You deny there is any truth to these accusations?"

"Absolutely, Mister President."

Cartwright looked at Elizabeth with hatred.

Good thing she's not a fire breathing dragon, Elizabeth thought. *I'd be a pile of smoking cinders if she were.*

"Mister President, the transcript of her transmissions will be in the communication room."

Elizabeth mentally crossed her fingers, hoping Stephanie had sent the transcript by now.

"I'd like to see that transcript," Hood said.

Adamski nodded his head. "So would I."

"Sir, I would like to see it also," Hopkins said.

"This is a trick," Cartwright said. "This woman hates me. She's trying to ruin my career."

Corrigan pushed a button. A door opened and an aide entered the room.

"Sir?"

"Go to the communication room and see if they've received something from Director Harker's unit. If there's something there, bring it to me. Be quick."

"Yes, Mister President."

The aide closed the door behind him.

"Director Harker, you are in serious trouble if your proof is not conclusive."

"I am not concerned about that, Mister President. The proof is undeniable. Her treachery explains why she has consistently blamed the Chinese for the events of the last weeks. She has done her best to point the finger away from the Federation."

"I've noticed the same thing," Hood said. "I thought it was odd when she accused the Chinese of trying to frame the Russians for Palo Verde."

The door opened and the aide came in. He seemed out of breath. He gave the transcript to the president.

"Is there anything else, sir?"

"No, thank you."

Corrigan began reading. He turned a page and looked up at Cartwright.

"Why, Ellen? Why would you betray me like this?" He tapped the papers with his finger. "You told the Russians everything that was going on in this office."

"That transcript is a fraud."

Corrigan shook his head. "No, I don't think it is. Some of this material was private to the two of us. I trusted you. You stabbed me and the country in the back."

Cartwright sprang to her feet.

"You bitch," she shouted.

She ran toward Elizabeth, her face twisted with rage.

Hood tripped her. Cartwright went down hard on her face, right in the middle of the Great Seal on the rug.

"Restrain her," Corrigan said.

Adamski was already up and pinning her hands behind her back. The Secret Service agent took Adamski's place, holding Cartwright down on the carpet. She kicked and screamed profanities. The agent spoke into his microphone and two more agents rushed into the room. They cuffed Cartwright and pulled her to her feet, still yelling and kicking. One of the agents grabbed her feet and pulled them up into the air. They carried her out of the office.

The door closed behind them.

"Well, if that don't beat all," Hood said.

CHAPTER 63

Nick, Selena and Lamont pulled up under the portico of Nicklaus' mansion. Black smoke stained the gray stone surrounding the entry. The doors stood open. The study where Nick had first seen Nicklaus was intact. The entrance to the elevator under the stairs was scorched and burned. It looked like the elevator shaft had acted like a chimney for the fire. Puddles of water and foam lay over the marble floor. The only signs of the battle in the hall were bloodstains on the stairs.

"Where do you want to start?" Selena asked.

Nick looked around. "They didn't find Nicklaus in the elevator. That means he made it up here. The question is where did he go after that?"

"He thought he'd triggered the war," Selena said. "He knew there wasn't much time to get to safety. Unless he was suicidal, he must've gone to ground. Probably somewhere here on this property."

"Gone to ground," Nick said. "Like he did when he was behind that desk and disappeared."

"His whole plan was to survive," Lamont said. "It's pretty hard to run things if you're dead."

"When Nicklaus dropped out of sight, he had to go somewhere," Nick said. "We only saw part of what's down there. There has to be more. I can't see him bunking down with the guards."

They went into the study. There was smoke damage on the walls and books. The desk still sat at the far end of the room by the window. The drapes on the window had been pulled open. Bright sunshine streamed into the room.

"Lot nicer with the sun coming in," Lamont said.

They went over and stood next to the desk.

"There has to be some kind of triggering mechanism," Nick said. "He was sitting in this chair."

Nick sat down in the chair. The desk appeared to be an ordinary wooden desk, if you could call a piece of furniture ordinary that was old and valuable. Intricate carvings of oak leaves and acorns ran around the top of the desk and down the legs to balled feet with claws carved into them. Drawers lined each side of the knee hole. The mechanism had to be somewhere easily accessible.

The top of the desk was polished walnut. An antique pen and ink set and a large green writing pad with leather corners were the only objects on the desk. Nick took out the pen and examined it. It was made of gold, heavy, with an old-fashioned sharp point. He set it back in its holder.

"There could be something in the carving," Selena said. "A hidden button, or something to push or pull."

Lamont stood next to Nick and the chair. Selena sat on one corner of the desk. Nick ran his finger along the carved edge under the desktop, over the leaves and acorns, feeling for anything out of the ordinary.

"It all feels the same. There's nothing obvious."

Lamont watched him. He pointed.

"That acorn there looks different."

"Which one?"

"That one." He pointed. "See how it's a little darker than the others?"

Nick looked where Lamont was pointing.

"You're right." Nick pressed it.

Nothing happened.

"Good guess, but it has to be something else."

He swiveled in the chair and his knee bumped against the side of the desk. The floor, the desk, and the three of them dropped down into darkness.

"Whoa," Lamont shouted.

Nick felt as though his stomach had jumped up to his teeth. He hung on to the desk until the platform suddenly slowed to a gentle stop.

"Damn, that was some ride," Lamont said. "Reminds me of a roller coaster I rode when I was a kid. It was called the Thunderbolt. Scared the heck out of me."

They'd ended up in a room. A row of lights marched down a hall leading away.

"My guess is we're back to level 20," Nick said.

"I don't see any sign of the fire," Lamont said. "I'll bet Nicklaus is here somewhere."

They hadn't brought the MP7s but they had their pistols.

"Lock and load. Safeties off."

CHAPTER 64

They started down the hall. There were dark spots on the floor.

Lamont bent down. "It's a blood trail. You hit him, Nick."

"Not hard enough."

They followed the trail and passed a storage room filled with barrels of water and enough food supplies to last for years.

"What's that electrical smell?" Selena asked.

Lamont pulled open a door. "It's coming from here."

An elaborate electrical panel with meters and labeled switches took up much of one wall. The rest of the space was taken up by stacked rows of heavy-duty batteries wired together.

"It's a solar set up," Nick said. "Looks like he's got enough juice to power almost anything. It figures. He'd need something to replace the loss of the grid."

"Nice set up," Lamont said. "Must've cost a few bucks."

"Let's keep moving."

Out in the hall, they kept following the trail of blood drops. They reached a T junction. A bloody handprint on the wall showed where Nicklaus had paused to steady himself. The blood trail led to the right. They followed it through a fully equipped kitchen and into an underground living room.

Nicklaus was sprawled on a white leather couch. Bloody smears stained the white surface. His white shirt had turned red. His breathing was harsh and shallow. He opened his eyes as they came into the room.

"Carter." He coughed. "You're supposed to be dead."

"As you can see, I'm not. Your plan didn't work out. There hasn't been a war, in spite of everything you did."

"It doesn't matter now, does it?"

He coughed again. A trickle of blood ran down his chin.

"You think you've won, don't you?" He said.

"Looks that way. You're dying, Nicklaus. Anything you want to say before they welcome you to hell?"

Nicklaus smiled. "I'll only be going home. Others will carry on the work."

"What others?"

"I'll show you. I'm sure they'd enjoy meeting you."

Nicklaus fumbled for a remote lying next to him on the couch. Lamont grabbed it before he could pick it up.

"Not this time," Nick said.

Nicklaus coughed. More blood trickled from his lips. He lifted his hand and pointed at a monitor on the far wall, then dropped back, exhausted. His voice was weak.

"Press the button labeled 'connect.' Go on, what have you got to lose? You need to introduce yourself. I want you to know who'll be coming for you. For you and your lovely wife and children."

He started to laugh, a cackling, bubbling sound. Suddenly he stopped. His eyes opened wide. He lifted his hand.

"Master," he said.

His hand fell back to his side. He let out a long, gargling breath and died.

Nick said, "Lamont, give me the remote."

"You're going to press that button, aren't you?" Selena said.

"I have to. You heard what he said."

"You sure, Nick?" Lamont said. "What if it's a trick?"

"I don't press it, we'll never know."

He pressed the button. The monitor lit. It showed a room with a large, leather chair. There was no way to tell where the room was located. The chair was vaguely European looking, expensive. A vivid painting of the phoenix rising out of flame hung on the wall behind the chair.

A man came into the room, wearing a dark red hooded robe. He sat down and looked into the camera. A Guy Fawkes mask concealed his features.

"You are Carter," he said. His voice was disguised electronically. "Since you are contacting me from the mansion, I assume Nicklaus is dead."

"That's right," Nick said. "Who are you?"

The man ignored the question. "You have interfered with our plan. There are consequences. You will regret your actions, I assure you."

"When I find out who you are you'll be the one expressing regret."

The Guy Fawkes figure laughed, the sound eerie through the electronic distortion.

"Brave words, Carter. You aren't going to find out who I am. People like me are out of your league. You have no idea what you've done."

"I think I have a pretty good idea. I've stopped you and your buddy Nicklaus from turning the world into a fireball."

"You have merely caused a delay. We will still have our war. We are Phoenix, Carter. We are the rulers of the world. We have always been the rulers and we always will be. Insects like you cannot be expected to understand why it is necessary for the cleansing to take place."

"What is it with you assholes?" Lamont said. "You think you can decide to have a war because it's what you want?"

"That is exactly what we think. We made a mistake in not wiping out your kind a long time ago. It won't be that way the next time around."

"My kind? Fuck you," Lamont said.

"It's hard to take you seriously if you're afraid to show your face," Selena said.

"Ah, the redoubtable professor Connor," the man said. "I don't think you would like to see what's under this mask."

"Why don't you try me?"

"I don't want to frighten your dear little children in the womb. One never knows how they might turn out. For that matter, one never knows if they *will* turn out. It's a dangerous world, Doctor Connor."

"You son of a bitch," Nick said.

"Now, Carter, sticks and stones and all that. This has been a very interesting conversation but it's time for me to go now. I would like to leave you with a bit of advice."

"I'll bet you would."

"Make sure you learn to look over your shoulder. From now on, you will never be alone."

The screen went dark.

"Jesus," Lamont said.

CHAPTER 65

Two weeks later, everyone gathered again in the loft. Ronnie was out of the hospital. He sat next to Burps on the couch. He scratched the big cat's belly and was rewarded with a rumbling purr.

Elizabeth cleared her throat.

"I have some bad news. There's no way to soften it, Corrigan has canceled our funding. We're shut down, effective immediately."

"That ungrateful bastard," Nick said. "Why?"

"The official line is that it's too much money to rebuild headquarters and replace the computers and equipment destroyed in the raid. He said we've entered an age of transparency and units like ours are no longer acceptable to Congress and the public."

"That's bullshit," Ronnie said.

"Yes, it is. The real reason is he's embarrassed by what we found out about Cartwright. We made him look bad. His Chief of Staff was a Russian spy. It doesn't get much more humiliating than that. It leaked and the papers are having a field day. He's getting even."

"Nice to know we're being rewarded by a grateful nation," Ronnie said.

"You wanted gratitude, you never should've joined the Marine Corps," Lamont said.

"I don't see the SEALS getting a lot of strokes, either."

Selena interrupted. "I think we should talk about how we go on from here."

Nick said, "Without government support, we're done."

"Not necessarily."

"What are you getting at?" Stephanie asked.

"You forget that I could fund the unit. That is, if we want to continue."

"It wouldn't be the same," Elizabeth said. "We wouldn't have official standing or presidential protection if something went wrong. Everything we do would be illegal. Besides, I'm tired. We've done enough. It's time to let someone else take on the crazies out there."

"There it is," Ronnie said.

"Then we're done? Really done?" Selena said.

They sat there for a moment, taking it in.

"I got an idea," Lamont said. "Why don't we think about it later? I say we celebrate. I've got a friend with a great nightclub. Let's rent the joint, invite our friends, and have a party."

"Good idea, bro," Ronnie said. "I might even have a drink with you."

"Make the call, Lamont," Nick said.

Later, when everyone had left, Nick and Selena were sitting together on the couch. Nick took her hand.

"At least I don't have to worry anymore about you putting yourself in harm's way. There was always going to be something."

"I know," Selena said. "I couldn't believe how hard it was to try and stay out of things. All that time when I kept thinking I wanted to quit, then when I had the chance I couldn't do it."

"The twins will be safe now."

"But what about this Phoenix group? I keep thinking about what that man said, about you always having to look over your shoulder."

"I've been looking over my shoulder ever since I can remember. Nothing much changes. He was trying to mess with our heads."

"I hope you're right."

"With the Project shut down, I don't know what I'm going to do with myself."

"We'll figure something out."

"We always do," Nick said.

Author's Notes

I like to base my stories on realities that exist in the outer world. One day I was looking at a picture of the Three Gorges Dam in China and wondering what would happen if it collapsed. It's a truly impressive structure, an amazing piece of technology. As told in the book, the reservoir behind the dam is the largest in the world. It holds an unbelievable amount of water.

The dam has known flaws. The weak point is found in the spillway tunnels under the dam. The design of the spillways and their location makes them susceptible to possible severe cavitation during an emergency release. All the critical functions of the dam are controlled by computers. All computers are vulnerable to being hacked, even those with the most sophisticated security. If this towering wall of concrete and steel were to fail, the results would likely be even worse than what I described in the book.

The new J-20 Chinese jet fighter is being built in a factory outside the city of Yichan, downriver from the dam. It would be destroyed in a collapse, along with all the rest of the new and critical infrastructure that the Chinese have placed there. Loss of life would be in the hundreds of thousands or more.

General Alexei Vysotsky's Directorate X is real and is in charge of technical/scientific intelligence and cyber security. To the best of my knowledge Section 5 does not exist, but something like it has to.

At the time of the Cuban Missile Crisis in 1962 I was still in the Marine Corps. I vividly remember a briefing where a map of Cuba was up on the wall. We were told to get ready for deployment. I remember thinking at the time that if war started there wouldn't be any Cuba left to deploy to. I still think that.

Submarine *B-59* was real, and so was the Russian captain's decision to launch nuclear tipped torpedoes at U.S. Navy vessels. At that time in the Soviet Navy the decision to launch nuclear weapons required agreement of the three most senior officers on board. The torpedoes never left the tubes because the second-in-command, an officer named Vasili Arkhipov, refused to authorize the attack. If those torpedoes had been fired, the U.S. would have retaliated and nuclear war would have begun. The result would have been massive mutual annihilation. Arkhipov's refusal to go along with his captain literally saved the world from destruction.

Nuclear tipped Iskander M missiles are currently deployed in the southeast quadrant of the Russian Federation as a deterrent to potential Chinese aggression. The Chinese have countered by moving Dongfen-14 ICBMs into the area. This is one of those potential nuclear flashpoints no one ever talks about. The Russians and the Chinese are not friends.

The Chinese proverbs quoted by Minister Deng and General Liu are genuine. A search of the Internet will reveal many such gems of wisdom.

We are now in the age of artificial intelligence, something that may not be good for human beings and other living things. If you've ever seen the *Terminator* series of films, you're looking at a Hollywood version of a possible future reality. A lot has happened in the field of artificial intelligence since the movies were made. The basic premise of the story, war between humanity and machines, is no longer as far-fetched as it might seem.

Many functions previously handled by humans are now being relegated to intelligent machines. Journalists gush over the possibility of robots having babies and robot/human hybrids. We're told that everything is going to be so much better because of robots and machines with AI.

AI computers such as Freddie or Merlin probably exist, although I doubt you and I will hear about them. Prototypes exist of robot soldiers who will replace humans on the battlefield. We all know about lethal drones. They are still guided by human operators, but that is changing. More and more functions of war are being handed over to machines. One day, wars will be fought by intelligent machines. Humans will be collateral damage.

In China, armed police robots are now on the streets. They are used for crowd control and look vaguely reminiscent of the robot policeman in the movie *RoboCop*.

Think about that for a moment. Armed robots now exist with the potential to make life-and-death decisions about humans. It's reality, not science fiction.

Welcome to our brave new world.

Alex Lukeman
2018

Acknowledgments

As always, my wife Gayle. It simply wouldn't be possible to write these books without her support.

Neil Jackson for creating wonderful covers for the books. Thank you, Neil.

All of the people who have written to me telling me how much they enjoy the books and how (sometimes) the books have affected their life. You know who you are and I deeply appreciate your comments. Thank you.

Last, but definitely not least, you the reader. None of this means a thing without you.

*****

If you liked this book, please consider leaving a positive review about it online. Reviews are critical to a writer's success, and I am no exception. If you didn't like it, please write to me at **alex@alexlukeman.com** and tell me why the book did not meet your expectations. I promise I will respond.

You can be the first to know when I have a new book coming out by subscribing to my newsletter. No spam, ads, or busy emails, only a brief announcement now and then. Just click on the link below. You can unsubscribe at any time...

http://bit.ly/2kTBn85

Made in the USA
Monee, IL
28 November 2019